# KING

## OF

Hyde Park

*Book 8 of the Kings of the Castle Series*

*Book 1 is the Introduction*

*Books 2-9 are standalones*

*Lisa Dodson*

Fiction Cove Publishing, LLC
Raleigh, North Carolina

*King of Hyde Park* by Lisa Dodson Copyright ©2023

Macro Publishing Group ISBN: (Ebook) 978-1-7331782-6-6 Fiction Cove Publishing ISBN: (Ebook) 978-0-9998917-5-9 Fiction Cove Publishing ISBN: (Trade Paperback) 978-0-9998917-6-6

www.lisadodsonbooks.com



Cover Designed by: J.L Woodson: www.woodsoncreativestudio.com
Interior Designed by: Lissa Woodson: www.naleighnakai.com
Editor: Lissa Woodson: www.naleighnakai.com

Manufactured and Printed in the United States of America

# KING

## OF

# Hyde Park

*Book 8 of the Kings of the Castle Series*


*Book 1 is the introduction*

*Books 2-9 are standalones*


*Lisa Dodson*

## ♦ DEDICATION ♦

For my Northwest Divas: Rena, Lisa, Christy, Deidra, and Tracey. We're proof that childhood friends do last forever!

To everyone that has encouraged me through the years to continue writing stories that inspire and entertain, I thank you. No matter what the beginning, you can always have a happy ending!

◆ ACKNOWLEDGEMENTS ◆

*My thanks to Naleighna Kai, for developing such an exciting, edge-of-your-seat world in which my fellow Queens of the Castle and I can play in! It was a blast!*

*Thank you also for your invaluable eye, amazing suggestions, and the sheer will to see your brainchild through to the end. Dro salutes you!*

# CHAPTER 1

"I think you killed him."

"No, I didn't," a deep-voiced man snapped. "The boss said to keep him out of the way. That's what I did."

"Yeah, but he hasn't moved in over twenty-minutes. I think he's dead," his partner repeated.

"Good thing it's not your job to do the thinking."

"Jonesy, Buster, the boss wants you both in his office," another man called from a distance.

"Coming," the big one named Jonesy yelled.

Buster stopped. "Do you think we should leave him?"

Jonesy didn't spare the man on the floor a glance. "He's knocked out. What's he gonna do? Besides, you wanna tell the boss why you didn't follow his orders?"

Buster grunted and then headed for the door. Their footsteps echoed on the concrete floor as they hurried down the hall. The moment the sounds grew distant, Victor Alejandro "Dro" Reyes opened his eyes and moved to sit up. The severe pounding in his head halted his actions. He didn't know what they'd injected him with, but his whole body felt like he'd been in a cage match and lost.

Short on time, Dro tried again to sit up. He had some difficulty because his hands and legs were tied. When he did manage it, his back protested, as did his stomach. After a moment, he recalled receiving multiple blows to his abdomen before another man had stepped in and shot him in the neck with a needle. After that, it was lights out.

His mouth felt like nothing had passed his lips in days. He shook his head to try and clear it. He'd been careless and should've known better than to separate from his team. Now he was on his own. If Lewis Wingate found out who he was, he'd lose his advantage. Luckily, he wasn't carrying identification, so his captors had no idea who he was.

Whoever tied him up had used zip ties to bind his hands. He maneuvered his wrists so that they were facing each other. A tattoo of a Lion's face in the center of three circles were imprinted on each wrist. The mane looked like flames, and in between the bottom of the two circle loops were nine spearheads. The art was a nod to the nine Kings of the Castle, his brothers-in-arms, who'd nicknamed him Dro. They had met at Macro International Magnet School, where Khalil Germaine had been their teacher and mentor. Each of them was from a different background, yet tapped by Khalil for the unique talents they possessed.

Right now, he could certainly use Daron Kincaid's help. He was one of the deadliest of all of them. Planning to take down an international crime ring was going to take all of the brothers working with laser-like precision. There could be no mistakes.

Dro snapped back to the present. He couldn't afford to get caught now. As the "Fixer" of the crew, it would derail all of the special projects he'd assigned himself to help with the Castle business. He pressed his wrists together once, twice, then held the third one for five seconds.

*Good. Help is on the way.* He just needed to get to the rendezvous point. Hauling himself up off the floor, Dro brought his hands up to his mouth. Catching the zip tie in between his teeth, he pulled it as tight as it would go with his hands facing each other and balled into fists. Next, he brought his hands above his head with his elbows wide open. Thrusting his arms down and away from each other in one quick movement was enough force to break the zip tie. Once free, he untied his legs.

Making his way to the door, he stopped at the entryway and listened. No sound. He wondered if it was a trap, but he didn't have time to waste. Failure to meet his men at the designated spot meant they would swarm the warehouse, and that would cause too much attention and drop a few bodies. Wingate's warehouse was located in a deserted area in an older part of Aurora, a suburban town about forty-five minutes west of Chicago. On a dirt road surrounded by lots of trucks and loading equipment, there was only one way in or out. To escape detection, his team parked their vehicles several blocks away.

The floorplans came in handy now as he moved along a wall, careful to keep his steps soft and even. Rounding the corner, he walked straight into the path of a guard. Startled, the man reached out to strike. With adrenaline pumping, Dro blocked the blow and struck the man rapidly with the edge of his hand, hitting the carotid artery on his neck and knocking him out instantly.

Grabbing the man, he guided him down to the floor before he fell and made a commotion. Next, he raced down the hallway and back toward the door he'd used to enter the warehouse. Heavy footsteps pounded the tiles, so he doubled back and went down a corridor with offices. The first two doors were locked, but he ducked in the third one and hid behind the door.

Taking a few deep breaths, Dro tried to fight off the nauseous feeling that threatened to double him over. Footsteps were headed his way. Shrinking back against the wall, he slowed his breathing and remained still.

The lights were off, so he heard, rather than saw, the doorknob turning. Slowly, the door creaked open, then light from the hallway lit a path into the room. Crouching down, he used his hands on the floor to keep himself steady, but the man backed out and closed the door behind him.

A full minute passed before he thought it was safe enough to leave. Opening the door, he stepped out.

"Wrong move, pal."

A forceful blow to the jaw sent Dro crashing to the floor. Before he had time to recover, he was hauled up again by the lapels of his jacket and slammed into a wall. This time, he saw the next blow coming and sidestepped before delivering a hit to the man's chest that sent him reeling back into the hallway.

* * *

Down the hall, two men were in a closed office having a heated discussion.

"I didn't sign up for this. You told me things were under the radar. Now I hear a man was captured and killed? I don't need that kind of publicity."

"Relax," the warehouse manager repled. "He's not dead. Not yet. But he was caught snooping around. I need to find out why. The boss ordered us to detain him, so he's detained."

"Who is this burglar? What did he want?"

"We'll find out soon enough. Anyway, that's not your concern. Are you able to move the shipment as we discussed?"

The other man shifted in his chair. "I'm working on it. I'm waiting to hear back from my contact in Cartagena."

"I don't need to remind you that time is of the essence, and my boss' patience is short."

Before his guest could reply, there was a loud commotion outside.

"What's that?"

"Stay here." The warehouse manager bolted from his chair and raced out the door.

Left alone, the man grabbed his briefcase and fled. He was still running when the skirmish down the hall caught his attention. That's when he laid eyes on the man thrown up against the wall. For a split second, he saw the one responsible. He recognized him instantly. *Alejandro Reyes.*

Letting out a gasp, he shrank back against the door as though he'd been spotted. Curiosity got the better of him, and after a few seconds, he leaned forward again for a peek.

Dro was on his attacker before he could recover, delivering a snap kick that caused his attacker's head to connect with the wall. Like a rag doll, he crumpled to the floor and was out cold. After that, he'd fled. Men were running every which way, shouting, barking out orders. Fearing for his life, he took off in the opposite direction. If Dro was here, that meant he probably had plenty of backup. That was all the incentive he needed to get out of there. He couldn't risk getting caught, or his plans would dissolve into thin air, and his life would be forfeited.

# CHAPTER 2

Racing back to his rendezvous point, Dro barely reached the exit when he heard men yelling for him to stop. Out of time, he rushed to open the door, but it opened before he touched the handle. Seconds later, he was grabbed by the arm and helped down the stairs.

"Thanks, Gray," Dro said, relief filling him when he spotted the head of his security team.

"No problem, sir," Grayson Daniels responded. "Can you run?"

He felt horrible, but he'd worry about that later. "You bet."

"Good," Gray replied, gesturing to the group of men speeding out of a side door. "Because we've got some company."

When his team took off running, he was right with them. Voices sounded behind them, followed by gunshots a few seconds later. Crouching lower, none of the men stopped running until they were clear.

All four members of his security team made it back to the black SUV parked a few blocks away. He didn't relax until the truck was speeding down Interstate 55 toward Chicago.

"Were you successful, sir?" Gray asked.

"Yes," Dro replied, trying to catch his breath. "I have what I need."

Gray nodded.

"Can I borrow a phone?"

One of the men handed one over. He dialed a number and waited.

Jaidev Maharaj, the King of Devon, and his physician answered on the second ring. He didn't waste time with pleasantries.

"Doc, I need you to run a few tests for me."

"Dro, do you know what time it is?"

"I was on a mission, and I got injected with something that knocked me out, but I don't know what. The syringe wasn't around when I came to."

The annoyance dropped from Jai's voice. "Stop by Chetan in the morning and I'll—"

"I need you to check me out tonight," Dro insisted. "The serum should've worn off by now, but I'm still feeling weak, groggy, and nauseous. I need to know what they put in me, and how much longer it'll last. Maybe you can give me something to counteract the effects?"

"Sure, if I can ascertain which toxin it is. I'm out the door right now."

"Thanks, Jai."

"Great, and Dro…hello to you too," Jai said with a chuckle.

"I'm sorry, thanks, man."

Next, Dro called Daron Kincaid. "Thanks for the tech. The tattoo came in handy tonight."

Daron was the King of Morgan Park. He helped the Castle out with high-tech security systems, as well as creating tracking devices that helped locate not just the other Kings, but child sex trafficking victims. He was also a fellow fixer of sorts and was used to Dro's lack of salutations. He said, "I noticed you activated the rescue beacon. I had already scrambled a team to your location, but Gray radioed that you were extracted."

"Yep, but thanks."

Daron laughed. "No problem, though I don't know why you didn't just use the earring. It's just as effective."

"I told you, the last thing I need is to explain to my parents why I got an earring at thirty-two years old. Trust me, getting beat up and my near-death experience was preferable."

They both laughed at that.

"I'm glad you're safe, Dro."

"Me, too," Dro replied. "I'll see you at the meeting tomorrow."

He hung up, passed the phone back to his guy, then closed his eyes for a moment. With all the projects he was juggling right now, the last thing he needed was to not be in peak form. He reached into a hidden fold that had been stitched into his pants just below the line of his belt. He closed his hand around the thumb drive he'd stashed there before he was captured.

Breaking into the foreman's office, Dro downloaded all the files he could find. He'd review them when he made it home and then pass them to his forensic accountant. Dro was confident that she'd find anything that was suspect. He needed evidence linking the activities of Lewis Wingate and Alistair Mayhew, Wingate's best friend and business associate to one of the former managing members of the Castle.

When he found that paper trail, he'd have the leverage he needed to squeeze information out of both of them to use to the Kings advantage. Dro would do what he excelled at best. He'd climb the ladder of suspects and dragging each of the men back down every rung, kicking and screaming if that's what it took. His goal? The man at the top responsible for giving his cohorts the green light to destroy the Castle. His gut instincts told him that they'd slip up and eventually lead him to the man in charge, and the one responsible for the attempt on Khalil's life.

Since he'd formed Vantage Point, Dro had painstakingly cultivated a network of allies from around the world. He was patient, he was methodical, and he'd find out what he needed to know. And right now, he wanted the name of the man who shot Khalil.

When he discovered it, there wouldn't be anywhere that man could hide that was safe from his reach.

"We're here, sir."

Dro opened his eyes to find them parked out in front of Chetan, the medical center Jai owned. He tried, unsuccessfully, to stifle a yawn. "It may be a while," he began.

"We'll be waiting for you," Gray confirmed.

He patted him on the back, then stepped out of the SUV and walked up to the front door which swung open before he'd had the opportunity to knock.

Jai stepped aside to let him past.

The two men were about the same height and build. Jai was East

Indian and only slightly darker in complexion than Dro. When they were together, both men received their fair share of feminine attention.

"You look terrible, Dro."

Dro managed a slow smile. "Thanks, I've been better." He followed Jai into an examination room. Knowing the routine, he hopped on the table and pulled his shirt over his head. He dropped it on the table but wasn't fast enough to stop himself from flinching from the pain.

Jai saw the bluish, purple marks forming above his ribs and across his chest. "You'll need an x-ray."

"No, I won't. They're not broken."

"Doctor's orders," Jai said in a firm voice as he wrapped a blood pressure cuff around his patient's arm.

*  *  *

Two hours later, Dro was sliding his shirt back over his bandaged ribs while Jai was writing notes in his chart.

"The good news is the bad guys knocked you out with morphine."

Dro stared at him. "That's good news?"

"Yes, in that it will wear off, and you're not going to become instantly addicted."

A few moments later, he handed him a brown paper bag.

"You know I'm not taking those."

"Dro, these are for the pain, which I know you're in, so stop being difficult."

He couldn't argue with that. Dro didn't subscribe to taking sensory numbing medication for every ache or pain. As a holistic healer, Jai shared his concerns and only treated his patients with homeopathic and Eastern healing modalities. That was one of the reasons he trusted him completely.

There was no point complaining because Jai would get his way, so all he said was, "How often do I have to take this stuff?"

"You'll want to take two tablets when you get home, and from there one as needed for pain."

He slid off the table. "Thanks, Jai."

"Dro, you know none of us are getting any younger," Jai warned, concern etched in his face. "And you're in the line of fire quite a bit—"

"Comes with the job, Jai."

"I know, but how long do you think your body is going to be able to handle all the pounding? Cracked ribs, dislocated bones, hand-to-hand combat—this stuff adds up, Dro."

"I'll be fine, doc. Thanks for patching me up."

"You may want to consider skipping the meeting tomorrow and resting up. We could get you the meeting notes."

"No," Dro replied, heading for the door. "I'll make it."

"That's the question of the day, Dro. For how long?"

# CHAPTER 3

"Alejandro, how dare you avoid me?"

"I'm sorry, Mr. Reyes. I tried to tell him that you were busy—"

"I don't need an appointment," Santiago Reyes snapped while eyeing Ellen Kiley, with disapproval. He stepped around her with an exaggerated swagger before switching to Spanish that he hurled in the general direction of his nephew.

Lowering the document that he was proofing, he stood and glanced at his administrative assistant. "It's okay, El, thank you."

She nodded and left his office, closing the door behind her with a firm click.

Santiago's tirade caused the opposite effect on Dro. As was his habit, he remained calm when his opponent was emotional. It gave him an edge when striking deals. Observing his uncle's tense shoulders, dour expression, and blotchy skin at the neckline alluded to his uncle's distress. Santiago appeared ready to combust, and the fact that Dro had yet to acknowledge his uncle's intrusion only increased the older man's agitation. Finally, he ended the deafening silence.

"Do not ever barge into my office again."

Santiago stood ramrod straight. "Then, don't ignore me when I summon you."

"Summon?" Dro drew out almost every syllable. "My parents are the only people on the planet that summon me to do anything—and you aren't either of them."

A phone call interrupted their conversation. Santiago strode across the room to the bar and fixed a Paloma, a tequila-based cocktail made with lime juice and grapefruit soda. He sloshed the ice around in his glass before taking a drink. Since it was the first time he'd stepped inside his nephew's office, Santiago walked around. The room was spacious, and though the walls were black, the windows with golden yellow fabric shades drawn up, doused the room in natural light. A massive oval mahogany wood desk was situated in the middle of the room, graced by a small glass vase with yellow-green flowers, a laptop, a folder, a large hourglass and a gold metal floor lamp next to the desk.

Agitated as to his purpose in coming, he slammed back half the drink in his glass.

The move caught his nephew's eye.

Sitting back in his chair, Dro gazed at his watch then back to his uncle. "A bit early in the morning for a drink, isn't it?"

Santiago ambled over to the seating area with three brown leather club chairs. He stretched his legs out in front of him and relaxed. A genuine smile curled his lips. "What's the saying? It's five o'clock somewhere?"

"You were rude to my assistant, and barged into my office, so I hope you're here for more than small talk?"

His uncle stiffened. "I wouldn't *be* here in the first place if it weren't for your shameless disrespect. I can't get you, or my brother to return my calls."

"You know papá is recuperating. The doctor said no stress."

"So now I'm stress?"

Moving to sit in the chair across from his uncle, he placed his feet up on a brown and white Houndstooth fabric ottoman, Santiago made a move to do the same until a glare from Dro waylaid those plans. Clearing his throat, he set his drink on a wood end table.

"This whole room is devoid of clutter."

"Just the way I like it."

Santiago chuckled. "Life isn't orderly. It's messy, complicated, filled with family, obligations, kids running around, chaos and love."

"Your point?"

"I watched you on the phone. You're always calm, your words measured and calculated. Does nothing ever rattle you?"

"I get paid not to be rattled, *tío*."

"That's not living life, *sobrino*, that's orchestrating it."

When he remained silent, Santiago continued. "I heard about Shawn Mayhew's run-in with the press, and that you've been asked to extricate him from his latest mishap. That boy is a bonafide train wreck."

"I haven't made up my mind on that … yet."

"Look, I never wanted our family to be beholden to Alistair Mayhew for anything."

"And yet, here we are."

"It was a sweet deal." Santiago shrugged. "How did I know it would turn sour and that Mayhew owned the lending company holding my loan?"

For a split second, his cool façade slipped. "You could've researched like every other businessman, or taken a moment to consider your options. Mayhew's made it clear that he'd take any opportunity to ruin our family. That alone should've made you reconsider."

"I said I didn't know it was him, plus I was desperate," Santiago stressed. "I needed this deal to go through to save my company. I'd tapped all my other resources, and the last thing I needed was big brother bailing me out—again."

"But big brother's sworn enemy is okay?" he shot back, moving over to the wall with two built-in bookcases. Leaning his hand on it, he gazed out the window. "There's a reason my father never did business with the man," he said after a minute. "He's a liar, dangerous, and never fails to screw over his business partners." Dro glanced over his shoulder. "You're no exception. Alistair won, uncle. He has you dancing to his tune, and now you're complaining because he wants to choreograph the steps?"

"I owed money, Alejandro." His tight grip on the armrest told of his anxiety. "To people that you never want to find yourself owing. I needed a win. A huge one. He was a necessary evil, and one I can handle if—"

"A necessary evil? And it never occurred to you that owing *that man* could be ten times worse for you, and our family? From the moment we relocated here, and he realized *Papá* wasn't going to do his bidding, he's wanted nothing more than our family out of Chicago."

"I know that," Santiago's voice lowered.

That whispered admission set him off. Returning to his desk, Dro sat down. "Now, I'm forced to save his son's good-for-nothing neck—and yours?" He roared in Spanish.

Santiago bolted out of his chair and went to face him. He slammed the glass down on the desk — the violence of his action spilling the grapefruit colored liquid onto the surface.

"How dare you speak to me like that," he snarled. "I'm still your uncle and command respect."

"Then save yourself," Dro countered with a dismissive wave.

He was about to return to work until his uncle pleaded, "This could be life or death for me." Santiago placed a hand over his heart as he fought back tears. "I've got a family. What will your aunt and cousins say if they learn that you had the opportunity to help me and you didn't."

"I doubt they'd be surprised."

His cell phone vibrated. Picking it up, Dro scanned over the message. His eyes widened, and he re-read the message. "What in the world?" He dialed a number. While it rang, he said, "Excuse me a moment," to his uncle.

"What do you mean there's been a press leak?" He demanded without saying hello. "There shouldn't have been any mention of it. Lola Samuels assured me that she'd handle it."

With his face growing tenser by the minute, Dro finally said, "I'll fix it," and hung up.

"What happened?" his uncle couldn't help but ask.

Too angry to censure himself, he blurted out, "There was supposed to be a media and press blackout about Khalil getting shot. I asked a PR contact to give us a few days to figure some things out before it aired. That's not what happened."

What irked him the most is that Lola had said she'd pull a few strings and make it happen. Dro had a low tolerance for any plans that went astray.

Picking up his office phone, he beat out an erratic cadence on the desk while he dialed a number and waited for an answer. He frowned when it rolled to voicemail.

"Lola, it's Alejandro Reyes. I've heard some very disturbing news. Somehow Khalil's shooting is now public knowledge. What in the world happened? I suggest you get this handled immediately or find someone else to sweep up the mess with Mayhew." He slammed the phone down and mumbled something under his breath.

"You *have* to help Mayhew," Santiago implored him. "And who is Lola Samuels?"

"Now isn't the time, uncle, and that's none of your business."

"If you don't help him, who knows what Alistair will do to retaliate," Santiago pointed out. "Can't you see this isn't just about you? It's about all of us."

"Again, something you should've considered before you got in over your head. You've been dancing with the devil for years now, uncle. The only thing that's different is he's changed the music and the tempo. Time's up."

Santiago turned pale. He crossed himself before saying, "I've said I'm sorry. What more do you want, my blood?"

Dro leaned so far over the table that he was almost nose-to-nose with his uncle. "If I thought it would help."

# CHAPTER 4

"There's no way I can work with Alejandro Reyes, and I don't care how good he is."

"Let me put it to you in a way you'll understand," Alistair Mayhew warned. "If you don't work with him to do damage control for Shawn, you're fired."

Lola recounted her discussion with her boss repeatedly in her head. She couldn't believe that she'd received an ultimatum: work with Alejandro Reyes, or she'd lose her job. The demand made her feel like she'd been pushed into the pool at an office function wearing every stitch of clothing she owned. All of her years of experience, impressive connections, and cache around town were important. They helped mold her career.

If she didn't manage to bring him back on her side, her hard-earned career at Mayhew Industries would go up in flames.

Hearing his annoyance at her not delivering on the media blackout she'd promised had affected her greatly. Receiving his scathing voicemail hadn't helped either. Lola had immediately called her media source and was dismayed to hear it confirmed that because of political interference, he'd gone back on his word to make sure that there was nothing mentioned in the local press about Khalil Germaine being gunned down at the Castle.

"I tried Lola, I really did. But I got the squeeze put on me first by an alderman, then by a Senator that I owed some favors to and—"

"Which one?"

"Uh-uh. I'm not telling you. I don't need you trying to hunt him down about this. Trust me, the less I say, the better—for all of us."

"That's not going to fly, Jerry," she countered, shifting to the offensive. "You promised me a full media and press blackout on Khalil."

"And I tried, Lola. I swear to you, but his pockets go a lot deeper than yours, as do his associates. I'm sorry."

Lola slammed the phone down and had to stop herself from hurling it across the room. She'd pissed off the one man that she needed to play nice with to keep her job. A perfectionist when it came to working, her word was her bond, and she always followed through on her promises. It didn't sit well with her that now Dro Reyes of all people had a reason to doubt her abilities. If Senator what's-his-name could unravel Jerry with just a phone call, she seriously needed to reconsider her alliances.

Irritation caused the back of her neck to prickle and her cheeks to grow warm. She was starting to rue the day Alejandro Reyes' name had even come up.

"Why do you have to be such a pain in my hind parts, Dro?"

Lola paced the floor of her Lake Shore Drive hi-rise apartment on the tail end of South Shore. Her socked feet were almost silent against the hardwood planks except for the dull thud from her tense stride. A booming clap of thunder sounded on the other side of her window, followed by the crack of lightning. She didn't bother to look up, which was uncharacteristic because she always enjoyed her view of Lake Michigan on Chicago's waterfront, even in the rain.

She had lived in the predominately African-American neighborhood for years and had never experienced anything but friendly people and courteous store owners and neighbors. It received its name from being located on the south lakefront. There were parks, a community garden, breathtaking views of Chicago. The area also had a reputation for being in rich cultural and architectural history, but it also carried its fair share of concerns about crime and overall resident safety.

Another boom of thunder announced itself. The weather echoed her mood today. She felt like she'd been hung out to dry with no clothespins.

Normally, Lola thrived on being up against impossible situations because she always found a way out of them. But this time, some easy answer wasn't going to fall out of the sky accompanied by cartoon bluebirds and theatrical songs or her can-do attitude. For the first time in her life, she didn't know how she was going to deliver.

Her boss had asked for some bizarre things in the three years that she'd worked for him, but this one exceeded even his eccentric expectations. When she'd pressed him about why Dro's company, Vantage Point, was the only one to help, he replied that Reyes was the best, and he wasn't leaving his son's reputation to chance.

It made sense, but shouldn't he have thought about that *before* Shawn created his latest scandal? Lola reasoned.

Several firms in the Chicago area specialized in crisis management. She'd met Dro in a professional capacity a few times and had heard nothing but the best about his work, but surely there had to be someone else who could satisfy her boss' request?

Besides, thanks to her misstep, he'd turned her down flat, and from his curt response, followed by a dial tone in her ear, that 'no' was final. Lola didn't beg anyone, least of all someone as cocky as Alejandro Reyes.

She thought about it for a moment. Cocky was a strong word. She didn't know him well enough to know whether he was arrogant or not. But one thing she did know was at the professional mixers where she'd glimpsed Dro across the room he'd carried himself with an air of aloofness and confidence that people couldn't fake. You either had it, or you didn't. And he had it. *Every single ounce of it.*

"Alejandro," Lola said aloud, then paused as if she expected something to happen. Then she said it three times like one was not supposed to do in horror movies. She shook her head and laughed at herself for being silly.

Lola almost hit the ceiling when her cell phone rang.

"Good grief," she gasped, holding a hand to her chest before taking a few slow breaths to settle her nerves then answering. She almost expected him to be on the other end of the call.

"Hey girl, what are you doing that's so important you couldn't call me back?"

"Trying to save my job," Lola muttered. She could've kicked herself the moment it slipped from between her lips.

The next ten minutes were spent explaining herself to her best friend, Michelle Johnson, who had a much bigger temper than she did, and the bite to match her bark.

"You want me to jack him up for you? I know people."

Lola burst out laughing. "I know you do, but no, that won't help me."

"It'll make you smile, though," Michelle countered, and she could imagine her friend's perfectly arched eyebrows wiggling with mischief.

"True, but I have to stay focused. I need Alejandro Reyes on my team."

"One thing you are, my friend, is resourceful. You always get what you want in the end."

Papers shuffling in the background, along with sounds that indicated the storm had made its way to her friend's area, caused Michelle to add, "I know you'll come up with something persuasive to get Mr. Reyes exactly where you want him."

She pondered it for a minute. Michelle was right. Lola Samuels was resourceful, and she would find a way to get him to work on turning Shawn's image around. Everyone had a pressure point. She just needed to find his.

* * *

Hours later, Lola was lying on the couch with her foot propped up on the back, staring off into space. Bypassing Jerry because she could've wrung his skinny neck, she'd called in another favor with an Assignment Desk Editor she knew at the paper. Her goal was to find anything she could use to get Dro on her side. Unfortunately, between her research and her friends, nothing turned up. Deciding to admit defeat, she picked up the phone and called Dro. The fifth ring echoed in her ear before he answered.

"I almost didn't call," she said after his greeting.

"I almost didn't answer."

She inhaled, tossed her legs over the side of the couch, and sat up. "Look, I know you're upset, and trust me," she said, pacing around the room. "I'm very sorry to have gone back on my word." Jerry's image sprang to mind. "But it wasn't my fault."

"Don't you control your actions and the promises you make?"

The question irked her. "Yes, I do," she replied stiffly. "But I can't control a Senator who has an ax to grind and is wanting to flex their influence muscles."

He paused for a moment before saying, "What?"

"Jerry, my contact. He promised that he'd make it happen. And he's never failed me before. After you called me, I contacted him to find out what the heck happened. He told me that first an alderman, then a Senator who he owed a few favors put pressure on him to make sure Khalil's shooting hit airtime."

A lengthy silence, then, "Their goal was to incite panic and sew discord at the Castle. If people think Khalil isn't up to the task that would undermine all he's trying to do to turn things around. What's the Senator's name?"

She returned to the couch. "I don't know. But Jerry did say that he's someone that you don't want to owe favors to," she said dryly. "Or his associates."

"Thanks. I'll call you later."

"Wait, what—"

"And Lola?"

"Yes?" She said, bracing for the worse.

"Thanks."

Dro hung up, leaving her staring at the phone in amazement. "What happened?"

# CHAPTER 5

"Are you sure it's him?"

"Of course," Dro replied, leaning back in his chair. "How many Senators do you know that have made very public criticisms of Khalil and what he's trying to do at the Castle?"

"Only one," Daron replied. "In addition to Alderman Knight, of course. Grant did mention there was a colleague of Knight's that had almost as bad of a reputation."

Grant Khambrel, the King of Lincoln Park, was an architect and owner of a multi-million dollar construction company that had landed a major contract with the United Center. He suspected that there were more than a few men in Chicago trying to find ways to unseat Grant's successful business.

"The Senator is a loud, aggressive man that's used to getting his way. I'm sure if I dig deep enough, I can find out where he has the bodies buried."

"After what you told me about his girlfriend, I'd caution you on spending too much time snooping around in his backyard," Daron advised. "We need you focused on other things."

We need to compare notes with Grant to see if they're the same guy. This one tried to show up unannounced at the hospital, and the Castle."

Dro's jaw clenched. "Did he get in?"

"No, at that point, police were still guarding Khalil and wouldn't let anyone in that wasn't family. He tried to throw his weight around, but he was asked to leave before my men escorted him out."

Dro stood. "I'll stop by the United Center and see Grant myself."

"If it's the same guy, we need to know what he's up to and with whom," Daron said. "Call me later, and I'll put a tail on him."

"Will do."

Valentina Reyes entered Dro's basement office with Travers on her heels. The man looked dismayed.

Dro smiled when he spotted his mother. None of the members of his family had any qualms about interrupting his meetings. It drove Travers and his assistant, Ellen crazy.

His mother was always welcome. His uncle was a different story.

Both men stood as Valentina walked over and kissed him on the cheek, causing Daron to chuckle when his buddy grinned like a kid at Christmas.

"Hello, darling. I hope I'm not disturbing—"

"Not at all, *Señora* Reyes," Daron replied, giving her a slight bow. "Dro and I were just wrapping up."

"Let me know," was all Daron said before he followed Travers out of the room.

"Why do they insist on calling you Dro?" his mother said with her lips curled up in distaste. Your name is Alejandro. It's a beautiful name and a family name."

"*Mamá*, it's just a nickname."

"Well, I don't like it," she protested. "I'd have a few choice words if someone tried to call me Val, or Tina."

He chuckled, remembering when his brother Raul's ex had called her Miss Tina." That was the last time they'd seen her at their house. "I'm sure you would." He tried to hide a smile. "Is *Papá* here?"

"No, he had a few doctor's appointments so he stayed home. Laura is going with him."

He paused at the note in her voice. "Is everything okay?"

"Yes, just routine," she replied, trying to perk up. "Just to make sure Victor's heart is well and that his blood pressure is normal."

He studied his mother a moment before nodding. Ushering her up to the first floor, they headed to the family room, where Dro claimed a spot next to her on the couch across from the pool table.

"Not that I'm not happy to see you, Mamá, but this is a surprise. Why didn't you tell me you were coming? I'd have met you at the airport."

"*Hijo*, I used to live here, you know." She smiled, her expression showing none of the worries he'd spotted earlier. "And I'm perfectly able to see myself from O'Hare."

"That's not the point," he countered, taking her hand in his. "I want to ensure that you are safe and comfortable, that's all."

She gave his hand a gentle pat. "I hired a driver to bring me here. Stop fussing over me. I'm *your* mother, remember?"

Properly chastised, Dro let it go. "So, what brings you here for a visit?"

"One of the local charities that we still support is having a black-tie event to raise awareness of human trafficking." Valentina reached into her purse and handed him an invitation. "We've given a large donation, but I'm on the board, so I like to show up for as many events as I can."

He passed it back. "I'll contribute as well."

She beamed with delight. "That's very generous. Every dollar raised puts us closer to bringing those guilty of exploiting others to justice and ending this horrible epidemic."

"When is the event?"

"It's tomorrow night."

"Are you hungry? Would you like to go out to dinner? Or I could cook for you if you like?"

She stood. "When don't I enjoy my son's cooking? Lead the way."

* * *

Scoping out the contents of his fridge, he made his mother one of her favorites, barbecued Galician steak with Chimichurri sauce, coupled with fried yucca and a generous salad.

By the time he had finished preparing their meal, Travers had set the table for them in the dining room.

"Nicholas, we could've eaten in the kitchen," Valentina gently admonished. "There's no need to go through all the trouble for just the two of us."

"No trouble at all, *Señora* Reyes," Travers said with a smile.

When he escorted his mother into the dining room, she let out a small exclamation of delight. Travers' version of "no trouble at all" was two table settings of her son's best china, candles, and a vase of freshly cut flowers from the garden.

A sly smile crossed her face. "Nicholas spoils you too much, I think."

"You know, I don't think that's possible," he said loud enough for Travers to hear.

Catching Travers sputtering before turning beet red, and hurrying out of the room, Dro let out a full-bellied laugh. Soon Valentina joined in.

"Anyway, nothing is too good for *mi Madre*."

"Well, *your mother* thanks you," she replied.

"So, how is your business?"

His fork halted midair. "It's fine. Why?"

"I'm just curious."

"Uh-uh," he countered, eyeing her with suspicion. Santiago's visit, and now her sudden appearance. *Coincidence? Not.*

"You're never *just curious* about anything," he continued. "Every question you ask is for a reason. I should know, I've inherited that trait from you."

Valentina placed her fork on the edge of her plate. "Has Santiago been to see you?"

*There it is.* Sitting back in his chair, he pushed his plate forward. Dinner was momentarily forgotten. He had a feeling he was about to lose his appetite. "Yes, he did."

"And?"

He took a sip from his glass of La Rioja Alta Gran Reserva, a red wine from Spain that paired well with the steak. "And what?"

"Don't play games, Victor Alejandro Reyes," she snapped. "Especially not one you learned from me."

# CHAPTER 6

His mouth curled into a lopsided grin. "Yes, he visited me, and yes, I plan to help him."

Valentina visibly relaxed. Dro's gaze narrowed on hers.

"I'm baffled at why you asked. It's not like I had a choice."

"There's always a choice, Alejandro. A right one, and a wrong one," she smiled sweetly, patting his cheek. "You chose wisely. There's nothing more important than family, *hijo*."

After dinner, he escorted his mother to the suite he'd allotted for his parents. The walls were covered in a soft gray paper with a pearlized floral pattern. The large four-poster king bed was a solid dark cherry wood that was balanced by plush, white bedding with gray fleur de lis along the border. Across the room was a sitting area with a dark gray suede sofa with a cherry red chenille throw and matching pillows. He had always loved the combination of soft and romantic, along with a bit of fiery passion from the red accents thrown in. Each element reminded him so much of his mother.

When his cell phone rang, he excused himself and stepped out into the hallway.

"Dro, it's Alexa."

"Hey, What's up?"

Alexa King was a woman he'd known for years. She was an expert in cybersecurity, counterterrorism, tactical and weapons.  She also owned an elite personal security firm, Dragonfly Security, that specialized in protecting women traveling on business to dangerous countries around the globe. They had collaborated on numerous assignments.

"I ran into a slippery little man named Burt Maguire in Barcelona. He can't hold his liquor or his tongue. We were surveilling a factory when a member of my team picked up on some chatter about an upcoming meeting. Normally, it wouldn't get flagged, but the name of a company popped up that I thought would interest you."

"Which one?"

"Wingate Industries."

"To what end?"

"Not sure."

"Thanks, Alexa. Can you keep digging? I need to know what he's up to."

"Will do."

She was about to disconnect the call, but he added, "Wait, do you know if Marena was successful in re-engineering her patient renewal formula?"

"Not sure."

"I'll call her."

He hung up and called Dr. Marena Dash. She was a scientist that he'd met through Alexa. The three of them had collaborated a few times on projects, and Dro had used her creations on several occasions. She was well-respected in her field, and he valued her expertise.

"Hey doc, do you have a minute?

"Sure, what's up?" Marena replied.

He explained Khalil's shooting, and though on the mend, his recovery was a slow process.

"I'm wondering about your progress with the patient renewal formula you created? If it could speed up his recovery time, that would help tremendously."

"It's a possibility, Dro. I'm working on the serum being patient-specific now. I find that aids the recovery process a lot better."

"Okay, I'll put you in contact with his team," he said before ending the call. He felt lighter. He wanted to do everything he could to make Khalil's rehabilitation easier.

Dro returned to find his mother out on the small balcony outside of her room. She was sitting on one of the chaise loungers admiring the garden and water fountain.

"I'm sorry about that."

"Business?"

"When isn't it?" he replied. "How long are you in town?"

"Just for a few days," she told him, settling onto the plush couch. "I couldn't come all this way to turn around a day later."

He sat on the edge of the ottoman. "I'm glad." He squeezed her hand. "I'm happy to have you all to myself. Shall I plan some activities for us?"

"Most certainly not," his mother retorted. "I'm here on a mini-vacation, Alejandro. I'm not one of those women that need every hour of their day filled with something. I'm busy enough at home with your father. No, I want to relax and enjoy a few days of leisure."

He couldn't recall the last time he'd had absolutely nothing to do on the weekend. Usually, he worked to catch up on paperwork. Now with the Castle business, he was also filling his time with covert operations like the one at Wingate's warehouse. Not that he would ever complain. He wasn't there for Khalil when it mattered most. That was not a mistake he would ever repeat.

After saying goodnight to his mother, he went upstairs to his bedroom. He turned on the water in the shower and was in the process of stripping off his clothes when he stopped. He sauntered over to his bed, sat on the edge and used the landline to call Lola.

He was about to hang up when she grumbled, "This had better be good," instead of a 'hello.'

"It is," he replied with a smile. A mental picture of what she could be wearing popped into his head before he could stop it.

"Oh, Dro," she sighed, then moaned. "What time is it?"

Something inside him stirred, and he quickly pushed it aside. He frowned and glanced at the clock on his nightstand. One O'clock in the morning. He had a bad habit of not noting the time when he called people. He just assumed if he was up, everyone else would be, too.

"It's late," he replied. "I'm sorry to call and wake you up."

"But."

He chuckled softly, "But, I just wanted to let you know that I've reconsidered about Shawn. I'll work with you to help clean up his act."

A slight shift of sound on the other end. "Are you serious?"

"Always."

"What happened to Hell freezing over the day you worked with me to help Mayhew?"

"You didn't notice how warm it was today?" he teased.

Silence ticked by before Lola answered, "Seriously, I want to know why you're going back on your vow."

"What you told me provided some valuable intel that helped me with another client. I want to repay the favor."

"Uh-huh," she said, sounding skeptical. She tried to speak, but a yawn came out instead. "Oh gosh, I'm so sorry about that."

He stifled a laugh. The thought of catching Ms. Professional in a few unguarded moments tickled him. "Not a problem. It's late. I really should let you go. How about we meet at my office tomorrow, I mean later this morning. Say nine?"

"Ten would be better. And my office."

Dro shook his head. He would've been on his third meeting of the day by that time. He shook his head and said, "Ten would be fine. I'll see you then."

"Wait, do you have my office address?"

"I can use Google like you did earlier when you were looking up information on me."

That statement caused Lola to gasp. "Wait, how'd you know that?"

"Ms. Samuels, it's my job to know everything," he replied calmly. "Goodnight."

She muttered the same before hanging up.

*Did I dream that?* Turning over on her back, Lola stared up at the ceiling. She yawned several more times while attempting to wake up.

"How did he know I did a background check on him?" she said aloud, then craned her neck as if expecting someone to answer. She laughed off her silliness and turned over on her side to get comfortable. She was incredibly happy that he'd changed his mind about their arrangement. It certainly made things much easier.

*Back to sleep, I go.* If Lola planned to match wits with Alejandro Reyes, she needed to be on her toes. Dragging due to lack of sleep wasn't going to cut it.

She allowed herself a full minute to congratulate herself on landing him as her temporary partner on the Mayhew assignment. When her time was up, she re-adjusted the covers and slid down further between the sheets. Closing her eyes, she said a prayer of thanks that Dro had finally come to his senses. She had a feeling that they would fit like hand and glove. Then the image of those chocolate eyes, muscular body, dark, silky hair, and dimples came to mind. An expectant sigh escaped her lips before she could stop it.

Pleased with herself, Lola was still smiling as she drifted off to sleep and back into the dream she was having with Dro as her leading man.

# CHAPTER 7

"Who do you think you are? You can't blackmail *me*."

Dro gestured to a full range of documents set out between them. "These ledgers say otherwise, Senator Davenport. Granted, I'm no expert, but I think you're siphoning campaign funds to make your pregnant girlfriend disappear. Literally," he added, "could be seen as a misuse of contributions—especially to the Federal Election Commission. And maybe to the police as a possible homicide, because as far as I can tell, she's dropped off the face of the earth."

"How dare you," Roland Davenport roared, now pacing around his spacious office like a caged animal. "I won't be bullied, and you can't prove any of the lies you're spouting." Then he stood ramrod straight as he sneered. "And for the record, I don't have a girlfriend."

"You mean that anyone knows about," he countered, his designer suit tightening around his slender frame. "Unfortunately for you, finding out information that no one wants to be known is what I do."

Senator Davenport stormed over to the table and shoved the mound of paper back across the desk. "Who are *you* in this town? A nobody," he snapped, with a dismissive wave of his hand. "I've certainly never even heard of you. So listen closely, *compadre*. I'm a member of the Illinois Senate. If you think I'm just going to kowtow to—"

"Who I am isn't important," he said, ignoring the blatant insult to his heritage. "The information I have, is. So if you want to call my bluff, go right ahead, but it will be a mistake that you'll regret for years to come. And you wouldn't want to…*kill* all those political aspirations you have, would you?"

The Senator's face turned ashen. Recovering himself, he was around his desk in seconds. He tried to push Dro back a few paces, but that wasn't possible since Dro had securely planted his feet.

"Don't you ever threaten me again, you understand me? I suggest you keep those preposterous lies to yourself, or I promise that I'll bury you."

In a split second, Dro yanked the man off his feet and had him sprawled across his desk. "That'd be an interesting trick. Now let me tell you what's going to happen. You are going to tell me what I want to know. You interjected yourself into my business when you tried to strongarm a subordinate into blitzing the media about Khalil Germaine. That was a mistake."

He tried to push Dro's hands away but failed. "Who's he to you?"

"Don't worry about that," he warned. "If I were you, I'd be more concerned about what I can do and who I know. And I promise you, Senator, if I get a hint that you've tried to get anywhere near Khalil again, or tried to use him to advance your endgame, I'll be the one to bury *you*." He lowered himself so that he was nose-to-nose with the man. "And it will take cadaver dogs to find you."

Spittle flew out of his mouth as Roland Davenport sputtered, but couldn't manage to put any words together. He shrank back from Dro's intense stare.

Dragging the man back to an upright position, he smoothed his shirt over his expansive belly, then patted him on the shoulder.

The Senator jumped liked a startled cat.

Sliding the papers back into a folder, Dro returned them to his briefcase and headed for the door. He stopped and looked over his shoulder.

"Do we have an understanding, Senator?"

Seconds passed as if the man were weighing the validity of his threats. In the end, rationale and self-preservation won out. He nodded and growled, "Yes, we do. Now get out of my office."

"It's been a pleasure," Dro quipped before walking out.

Travers was waiting for him at the curb. "Everything went well?"

"Of course. Senator Davenport was happy to see me."

Travers arched an eyebrow. "I find that hard to believe."

"Come on." He grinned. "Would I lie to you? He *was* happy to see me…leave."

Travers laughed.

Throwing the briefcase across the back seat, he climbed in the back of his black Mercedes SUV. Travers trotted around to the driver's side and slid behind the wheel.

"Miss Samuel's office?"

"Yes." Glancing at his watch, Dro frowned. His meeting had run longer than he'd expected. "We'll make it on time, won't we? I dislike being late."

Travers looked at him in the rearview mirror. "I'm well aware. It's almost as reprehensible as men wearing Sperry's with shorts and a sweatshirt in the middle of winter," he grimaced. "It's a bloody disaster."

* * *

Lola smoothed her hands over the royal blue square neck sheath dress draped across her curvy body. It was the first time she'd worn cap sleeves. She always thought the cut made her arms look big, but Michelle, who had done a quick video chat, assured her that she looked fierce. Her shoulder-length, brown hair was swept into a messy bun with wisps framing her face. Running late, she'd grabbed her black tortoiseshell glasses instead of contact lenses.

In need of an extra boost of confidence since getting off on the wrong foot, Lola made sure that her hair, makeup, and outfit were firing on all cylinders. She peeped down at the blush Ferragamo pumps. From the moment she'd spotted them in a magazine, she'd loved them. She'd commented to her mother how beautiful they were.

Lola was genuinely surprised months later when her mother, Maggie Samuels, presented them on her birthday.

"Mom, these shoes are almost half the rent on my apartment."

"Yes, they are," her mother had observed with a wide smile. "But you're our only daughter, who else do we have to spoil?"

Lola couldn't argue with that logic. Besides, she didn't want to. She loved her parents. She loved her shoes. Though she'd only worn them three times, this being the third. She knew it was crazy, but she always felt like nobody could say no to her when she wore them. She called them her Cinderella heels.

The intercom buzzed on her desk phone.

"Mr. Alejandro Reyes is here to see you, Miss Samuels," her assistant Jess replied.

"Thanks, Jess, show him in."

A moment later, she ushered Dro through the door. Jess stood aside as he sauntered in.

Lola was standing by the window, so she had to walk across the full length of her office. He didn't appear to be in a hurry, so she took her time, too. It gave her a moment to appreciate how good he looked dressed in a dark gray suit, blue and white striped shirt, a dark blue silk tie, and black shoes. He exuded so much masculinity he could've poured it into a cup, and she would've happily sipped every drop.

Her assistant gazed at him, and then to Lola. She mouthed the words, *"Oh my gosh."* Held her hand to her forehead as though taking her temperature and faked a swoon.

Lola had to work hard not to burst out laughing. She gave her assistant a stern stare before she said, "Thank you, Jess."

"My pleasure, Miss Samuels. Shall I hold all your calls?" She asked, trying to linger.

"Yes, thank you."

"Of course," she stressed before turning to leave. She stopped short, almost throwing herself off-balance in the process. "Would you care for some coffee, Mr. Reyes? We also have tea, soda, bottled water?"

He turned around and gave Jess his full consideration. Lola noticed that her assistant looked as though she would truly pass out from his undivided attention.

"I'm good, thank you, Jess," he said with a lazy smile.

Her assistant stood there a full three seconds as if she'd forgotten her name.

Lola's eyebrows crept into her hairline. "Jess?"

"Hmm? Oh, sorry about that." She blushed and laughed at herself as she hightailed it out of the room, closing the door behind her.

Lola could understand Jess' momentary lapse of professionalism. It had been a while since she'd seen him in person. If at all possible, her memory hardly did him justice. Even with her heels, he was taller, and she was five feet, ten inches.

It also caused her a little embarrassment to know that her "dream" Dro was almost spot on with the man in person. His dimples, the flecks of gold in his brown eyes, even his luscious mane of thick, jet black hair was jaw-dropping.

Lola had to keep her hands fisted at her sides to stave off the desire to touch the wisps of hair falling across his forehead.

He had the kind of looks that caused a woman to place a hand over her heart without even being aware she'd done it. And his voice only added to his appeal. Dro never rushed to do anything, especially not to speak. He was reserved, and always calculating with his words. And he had the fiercest poker face she'd ever seen. He never gave away what he was thinking. He was notorious for it.

Clearing her throat, Lola said, "My apologies, please, have a seat." She motioned to the conference table in the corner.

He followed behind her and pulled out her chair before taking a seat himself. He crossed his leg at the ankle and unbuttoned his jacket in one fluid motion. He motioned for her to begin.

Her office phone buzzed.

"Excuse me for a moment," she said walking to her desk. She picked up.

"Yes, Jess?"

"Oh my gosh," Jess gushed. "Did you notice that he looks just like that singer, El Debarge? From back in the eighties when he was—"

"Thank you, Jess. Yes, please reschedule that meeting for another day."

"Huh?"

Hanging up, she rejoined Dro at the conference table. "Sorry about that. I thought I'd start with a quick background on my work here—"

"No need," he interrupted. "You've been working at Mayhew Industries for a little over three years now. You beat out hundreds of applicants for the coveted position as Director of Public Relations. Before that, you worked at a boutique PR firm across town, as director, and before that, a firm in Evanston as a junior partner. You left both when you were passed over for promotion in favor of your white, male counterparts. You graduated at the top of your class from the University of Illinois at Urbana-Champaign." He casually crossed one leg over the other. "You're originally from Alexandria, Virginia, where your parents still live. At least half the year. They have a condo here in Chicago not far from you in the Gold Coast neighborhood. You're an only child, never married, no children, or pets."

Lola took a few seconds to process how he had summed up her life. "Are you going to tell me about my financial investments, too?" She joked.

"Do you want me to?"

# CHAPTER 8

Lola stared at him, unable to tell if he was kidding or not. She decided he wasn't.

"You're very thorough, Alejandro," she said, stiffly resorting to his full name.

"You wanted the best, Lola," he said with an arresting smile. "You've got him, and like I said before, call me Dro. My friends do."

She longed to wipe the smug look off his face, but she couldn't afford to. "Oh, we're friends now?" she asked, mentally kicking herself because she'd already been calling him Dro in her mind. Alejandro sounded official, but Dro sounded more … dangerous.

"I'd say we're past the colleague stage, he declared. "Remember, I've heard you moan in your sleep."

"Wait a minute," she started, but then stopped. She'd been so tired the night he called that she could hardly discount his claims. Her face grew warm at the remembrance of her dream. Instead, she said, "Moving on."

Dro was notorious for his thoroughness. That quality was one of the main reasons Alistair demanded him, but now that attention to detail was cast in her direction, and it was uncomfortable. His invasiveness left her feeling like he'd caught her dancing around her apartment in her underwear.

When she glanced up, it was to find Dro staring at her with an inscrutable expression. Lola's gaze connected with his for a few moments before she turned her attention to her desk. Her finger trailed the length of her eyebrow as she struggled to focus. Putting her personal feelings aside, Lola opened up the folder on Shawn Mayhew.

"Shall we begin?"

* * *

An hour later, Lola tossed that same envelope aside in disgust. Dro had shot down every one of her team's ideas. *So much for you having your Cinderella heels on and nobody telling you "no."* She was ready to change fairytales and click her heels three times and go home. He'd said "no" so often she wondered if the man said "yes" about anything.

"You think I'm difficult," he stated, his dark brown gaze narrowed on her.

"The thought had crossed my mind."

He leaned forward, the fabric of his shirt stretching tightly across his muscled chest. "Lola, none of these strategies are going to work because they're disingenuous. It's like you're announcing to the community, here comes the bad boy going out of his way to make people like him.

This whole proposal feels like we're doing one continuous photo-op."

She neglected to tell him that Mayhew had approved all of their ideas.

As if he read her mind, he said, "If this is going to work, we cease making Shawn appear like a wonderful guy, when he's not. It can't just look natural, Lola. It has to *be* natural."

She knew that, but each of her attempts to steer the team in that direction had been shot down by Alistair. He wanted to throw money and the paparazzi at the problem until Shawn's image cleaned itself up, or people forgot he was caught partying with an underage young woman in the VIP section of his favorite nightclub. And that was just one of the seemingly weekly dilemmas Alistair's offspring found himself embroiled in.

Too much attention was placed on his misdeeds and by extension, his father. That's when Alistair summoned Lola to his office and demanded she "handle" the situation. Dro had already stated that if the circumstances had been any different and that video hadn't cleared Shawn in some way, he wouldn't touch this assignment in no shape, form, or fashion. He took that kind of lacivioius behavior with minors very seriously. So did she.

"Lola?"

She stopped daydreaming and gave him her attention. "I'm sorry, Dro. You're right, and I agree. Shawn should be doing more around the community, but not just so the media can take pictures and interview him. He needs to give back and help the people of this city."

"Exactly, and I know the perfect place to start."

By the time Dro finished his idea, Lola was smiling and jotting down notes.

"He won't enjoy it, but I love it," she replied. "I didn't know you volunteered."

"Don't sound so surprised," he countered, his infectious smile back in place. "I've been a part of the Chicago Mission Relief Center and Hyde Park Community Center's Young Entrepreneurs program for years. Vantage Point sponsors a youth basketball team and provides supplies to several of the after-school programs around Chicago. I also provide my services to help a friend of mine, Reno DeLuca. He runs a center for women who are victims of domestic abuse."

She was aware that Mariano "Reno" DeLuca, was the King of Chatham, and a successful architect and businessman. His brainchild, The Second Chance at Life Women's shelter, was a beacon of hope in a neighborhood plagued by gang violence and drug activity. "Two of my brothers, Reno and Daron, provide extra men on rotating shifts to help with security at the facility."

"That's impressive," Lola responded. "I volunteer, as well. I think it's very important to help our youth. Preparing them for the super competitive job market is a necessity. Heading Mayhew's charitable foundation is one of the things I insisted on before coming on board."

* * *

Dro pondered that statement. It made him wonder how donations given to Mayhew's foundation were being funded. Was it to aid money laundering orchestrated by a few of the managing members? Was Lola aware of any of the man's side ventures? He would watch her closely to see if she led him to any new information he could use against Mayhew.

The thought that Lola could be a willing participant in Alistair's shady business dealings caused him to blow out a harsh breath.

Lola glanced up immediately. "Are you okay?"

He could've kicked himself for the emotional outburst. Frustrated, he blurted out, "How about a tour?"

Caught off guard, Lola said, "Um, sure." She pushed aside her laptop and stood. Smoothing her dress, she motioned for the door. "Follow me."

Not one for impromptu moves of any kind, he surprised himself by voicing that thought aloud. He was committed now, so he'd go with it. Bringing up the rear, he tried his best to concentrate on committing every detail about Mayhew's establishment to memory, and not the rhythmic swaying of Lola's hips as she walked.

* * *

"This is the executive floor, so Mr. Mayhew, the company's officers, legal, marketing, and accounting are up here."

"Where's Mayhew's office?"

Lola switched directions and led him there instead. After opening Alistair's door, she walked in with Dro following.

"Normally, he's in, but he had an off-site meeting today."

Moving around the room, Dro took everything in. He noted the camera mounted near the ceiling. He walked over to the window and peered at the Chicago skyline. It was a sunny day, which afforded him a birdseye view that spanned miles out, Lake Michigan and Navy Pier.

"A million-dollar view for sure." When he turned around, he made a sweep of Mayhew's entire desk, making a show of admiring the personal pictures.

"What about his son? Will I get a chance to meet him while I'm here?"

"Oh, he doesn't have an office."

"On this floor?"

"No, in general," she clarified. "Shawn doesn't work at Mayhew."

"That's odd. Why wouldn't Mayhew's only child work at the company his great-grandfather founded in the early nineteenth century?"

Lola waved away that thought. "From what Mr. Mayhew has told me, his son doesn't have a head for business."

He leaned in to grab a picture off Mayhew's desk. As he did, he quickly scanned the neat stacks of papers on the desk before returning the picture to its original spot. "Don't take this the wrong way, but if that's the case, why am I here?"

"To help us clean up Shawn's image. Though he's not working here at Mayhew, he's still a Mayhew. Which means that any publicity generated by a family member is bound to hit the papers. Mr. Mayhew wants to make sure that the company's image, and by extension, his family's, is always positive."

He glanced at his watch. "I'd better get going. I have another meeting across town in an hour."

"Oh, of course." She extended her hand and he accepted it into his much larger one. "Thank you, Dro."

As if trying to read her mind again, he said, "You're welcome, Lola."

"Do you have a moment to set our next meeting before you leave?" She asked as she walked him to the elevator lobby.

"Sure, if we're quick."

"Great. How about Thursday?"

He shook his head. "I'll be out of town. Friday?"

"I'll be working from home that day," she informed him. "There's a guy coming to provide an estimate on getting my floors refinished."

"I'm out of town the next week, so how about I come to your place?"

"Pardon me?" The words slipped out before she could stop them. Her skin at her dress neckline grew warm. "No offense, that just caught me off guard."

"None taken. I just thought it would make sense to meet you there so we can move forward. You can begin work on Shawn's re-vamp while I'm out of town."

"Yes, of course," she conceded. "I'll text you my address."

"No need," he replied with a devilish smile.

# CHAPTER 9

"You're late."

"I'm never late," Dro corrected.

Shaz glanced at his watch, then back to his buddy. "Were you in a different timezone when you scheduled this meeting?"

He slid a folder across Shaz's desk and took a seat. Ignoring the barb, he observed Shaz as he read over the contents in the folder. With waist-length locs, medium brown skin, and a chiseled, muscular body, he looked ready to take his place on the cover of a Men's Fitness magazine. Chastising himself at his folly, and the fact that he hadn't had time to hit the gym in over a week, he waited for Shaz's reaction.

After some time, his friend glanced up.

In full lawyer-mode, Shaz said, "I know I don't have to remind you that the bugs you planted in Wingate's warehouse weren't legal, nor was breaking in to obtain stolen data files from his computer?"

"Technically, I didn't break anything," he ventured. "Okay, except maybe one guy's nose."

"Dro—"

"Yes, I know. Don't go all Perry Mason on me, Shaz," he protested. His hands stretched out in front of him in mock surrender. "I realize none of this is admissible in court, but that wasn't the point."

"You were on a fishing expedition."

"Exactly. And this proves I hit the mother lode." He tapped his finger on the edge of the thick ecru-colored folder. "This is way better than just knowing about Lewis Wingate's corrupt activities, Shaz. He's done my homework for me. It's all there in print. I have Alexa King following a lead she discovered while in Barcelona. I don't know what it'll turn up, but it's always best to have more ammunition then you need."

"Especially you," his friend retorted.

"Not only can we follow the trail of breadcrumbs to his crooked business dealings, but it implicates a few of the former members who tried to run the Castle into the ground. We've got meeting dates, agendas, merchandise shipments, even dirt on a few local officials."

"But Dro, you can't use any of it," Shaz reminded him, rubbing a hand across his neatly trimmed beard.

"That's true, but my goal wasn't to use this in court. No offense, but I don't need these guys and their millions to tie our hands with the proverbial red tape."

"I know how this works. Ace lawyers on the take, no offense."

Shaz grinned as he crossed his massive arms across his chest. "None taken. You know how I feel about corruption in the judicial system."

"Anyway, this isn't about going through the proper channels to get things done. I want to know where the bodies are buried, Shaz," he gestured to the documents. "Pictures, dates, names, shipment manifests. This isn't about chopping off a rung of the beanstalk. It's about getting the whole thing, plus the giant at the top."

"A little whimsical for you, isn't it?"

"True, but you see where I'm going with this. I want to make certain we inflict the maximum damage to this cesspool of corruption and not just some spanks on the hand that will allow them to move and set up camp somewhere else. The same way they tried to do after we shut down their child sex trafficking outfit."

Shaz let out a long, slow breath. "I get that, but we have to tread carefully, my friend. Things could've ended a lot worse the last time you tangled with Wingate. Dangerous men do dangerous things when cornered."

Dro inched forward in his chair. His expression barely contained the anger he felt. "We all knew when we signed up for righting the wrongs at the Castle that things were going to get dirty. The men we're dealing with didn't play by the rules when they came for Khalil and Vikkas. They could've died, Shaz."

"I know, Dro," he said in a resigned whisper, settling back in his executive leather chair.

"Then you know how this has to end. We don't stop until we get justice for Khalil, the Castle is safe against all threats, foreign and domestic, and those who would do mortal harm to the nine Kings are stopped."

"Bro, I'm with you." Shaz tapped his closed fist on his hand. "You know that. But I'm bound by the rule of law. I can't step outside of those parameters. No matter how deserving someone is."

"Well, I can—and will."

Shaz threw up his hands. "Better not tell me the details, man. I mean it."

"Do I ever tell *anyone* the details?"

He chuckled at that. "Fair enough." He continued scanning the documents. "So, how's working with Lola going? You two got off to a rocky start."

"It's better than expected." An image popped into his head of Lola wearing the snug, blue dress that hugged her body's curves in all the right places. And the pumps that made her legs seem like they were a mile long. He pictured those legs wrapped around him in the most delectable ways. That image made him swallow hard. Giving himself a mental shake, he focused on their conversation.

"I don't foresee any problems collaborating if that's what you mean."

"That's because she's not aware you're trying to pump her for information."

Something in Shaz's tone caused him to take it as a double entendre. *Madre de Dios, those heels again.* He had to get it together.

Standing, he walked over to the window to give himself something to do. Each storefront had an identical black awning with the store name written across the top. There were large black planters filled with plants and placed strategically down the block. Being predictable held a certain calm, but in certain situations, could be deadly.

"Dro? Did you hear me?"

"Yes," he finally managed to say. "And, I've done no such thing. My gut tells me Lola is my ticket to finding Mayhew's weaknesses and exploiting them."

Shaz placed all the papers back in the folder and laid it next to Dro's briefcase. He joined his friend at the window and thumped him on the shoulder. "A friendly word of advice?"

"Sure, counselor."

"Don't play with too many fires, Dro. I don't want to see my best friend burned."

A wide grin shot across his face. "You know I don't have a low switch, Shaz. Burning hot is all I know."

"If Lola finds out you're using her to bait Mayhew—"

Dro waved off that notion. "Relax. You worry too much. I always play ten steps ahead."

"Yes, but you've never had this queen on your board before. From what I hear, she can hold her own with the best of them."

Leaving Shaz's side, he slid the folder back into his briefcase. "I *am* the best of them," he countered before waving goodbye.

"Being the cockiest doesn't make you the best."

Dro shut the door, but could still hear Shaz's raucous laughter as he walked past the reception area and out the front door.

* * *

"This whole idea sucks."

Lola tried her best to keep her face neutral. Shawn was plucking her last nerve. The man was as whiny as his father was demanding which wasn't a good look for either Mayhew.

"It may suck, but your alternative is court-mandated community service."

"How was I supposed to know she was underage?" His expression shifted into a wide grin. Did you see her—"

"Please focus," Lola interrupted, not interested in his umpteenth recitation of the girl's body attributes. "You need to take this seriously. Your only saving grace was her post on Social Media about duping you into getting her into the club. Trust me, the judge didn't have to go light on you."

Shawn had worn a disinterested expression for the entire conversation. "So?"

Lola closed her eyes and tried to count to something that wouldn't result in her smacking him upside the head and getting fired.

"So, we are going to do what your father asked. He wants us to help improve your image, and that's what we're going to do."

He sighed dramatically before throwing his hands up. "This is boring. Surely, you can come up with another way? Just tell my father that I've already done all this stuff."

"That's not going to work this time, my boy."

Both of them turned to see Alistair standing just inside the door of Lola's office.

He was a tall man, but he wasn't in shape and had that middle-aged spread. His hair that was once dark was mostly gray, but he kept it cut in a flattering style combed back from his face. Lola thought his dark blue gaze was always intense as though he didn't miss anything. Overall, he was a good-looking man. However, in her opinion, he scowled too much.

"If you can't cut it, you'll be on the next flight, coach that is, to your uncle's Mission in Honduras."

That threat caused Shawn's feet to drop from the top of Lola's desk and back to the floor. Turning, his blue eyes, so like his father's, held a trace of fear.

"Dad, you wouldn't," he protested. "That place isn't safe. What if I'm kidnapped and held for ransom? I could die."

"Or you could grow a backbone and stop acting like a toddler in nappies."

Shawn's face contorted with anger. He ran a hand haphazardly through his dark blond hair setting it on edge. "I'm serious."

Alistair didn't give an inch. "So am I. My entire PR team is working indirectly to make sure that you do what you're supposed to do. And do you know what indirect means, son?"

"Yes, father, I'm not an imbecile," Shawn sulked, sitting up taller in his chair. His slim figure was ramrod straight. "It means they're not billable."

Despite his frustration, Alistair smiled. "Very good. That's correct, which means that your little tantrums are costing me a fortune. So make your choice." Alistair sat on the edge of the desk so that they were eye-level.

"Turn yourself into a model citizen and get the press off our backs, or you, a bundle of mosquito netting, and a month's supply of bug repellant are headed out on the next plane to Central America."

The two Mayhews regarded each other. Lola couldn't believe she was in the middle of the standoff. She was about to complain that she didn't get paid enough for this foolishness, but then reality kicked in. She did.

Shawn's expression soured. "Community service."

"Great." Alistair turned to Lola. "He starts tomorrow. Time is money, Shawn. Let's go, so you can stop wasting both of mine."

Father and son stormed out of her office, plunging the room into grateful silence. Lola dropped into her desk chair and let out a loud breath. Spinning her chair, she gazed out of the window. She was expecting to see storm clouds based on the events of the last few minutes, but outside was sunny and clear.

Her thoughts turned to Alejandro Reyes. She pictured him making some high-powered deal while on the tarmac in his private jet. He was sipping San Pellegrino with a lime wedge while some stuffy older looking man wrote a check with a ridiculous amount of zeroes and handed it to him. In her mind, he almost looked bored as he thanked the man before having him escorted off his plane.

"What a life," Lola said dreamily. "Now that's how you do it."

# CHAPTER 10

"See, that's how you do it," a man slapped his friend's back. "Show him we ain't punks."

Nodding, the man threw another punch that connected with Dro's midsection and one to the jaw. They high-fived each other as he crumpled to the floor.

The metallic taste of blood caused him to spit onto the dirty, wood floor. He wiped the back of his hand across his mouth and was slow, but managed to get back on his feet.

"I suggest you leave *suit*," he spat out. "Before we have to get rough."

"Oh, I'm leaving," he assured him. "And I'm taking my client with me."

"That ain't happening, *amigo*." The man pulled a gun from the back of his waistband. "She's mine, and I'm not sharing—at least not with you."

His buddy chuckled and hit him on the arm. "You got that right."

While he was talking, Dro moved to stand between the gunman

and his girlfriend. "Tell you what." Taking a quarter out of his pocket, he placed it between two fingers. "If you can knock me out before this quarter hits the ground, you win. I'll leave, and your girlfriend stays with you."

The woman standing behind him let out a soft exclamation. He glanced over his shoulder and saw her stricken expression. Her eyes filled with unshed tears. Smiling at her reassuringly, he turned his attention back to the two men standing a few feet in front of him. "But if I can knock you out in the same amount of time, I win, and she and I walk out of here without any trouble," he explained.

He could tell by the flickering gaze and furrowed brow that the man was weighing his options. "Come on. You aren't scared of one suit, are you?" He goaded.

"Deal," the man replied, returning his gun to the back of his pants. His muscular arms flexed a few times as he prepared himself.

His friend, a burly man wearing a pair of jeans that sagged beneath his belly that was covered by a sleeveless basketball jersey, stood right by his side. "Piece of cake."

"One, two, three." Throwing the coin up in the air, the first blow Dro delivered was to his loud-mouthed friend. He punched him on the chin, and it was lights out. He reared back and dodged an uppercut the boyfriend tried to deliver before sweeping the man's feet out from under him. Next, he followed up with a powerful scissor kick to the man's abdomen. The quarter landed on the unconscious man's chest. He bent down and retrieved it.

"How'd you do that?" the woman whispered behind him.

"Lots of videos," Dro joked, sliding the quarter back into his pocket. No need to tell her he'd started training at Khalil's insistence back in high school.

Taking her by the arm, he reached down with his free hand and retrieved her suitcase. His hand was almost on the doorknob when a bullet whizzed by him, followed by, "You open that door, and you're dead."

As if to prove the point, the boyfriend rushed over and pressed his handgun to the back of Dro's head. "I told you, she's mine, and that's how it's going to stay. If I gotta kill you to prove my point. Well, that's how it goes, homey."

Dropping the bag, Dro released his hold on his client and raised both hands in the air.

"You don't want to do this," he warned. "Trust me."

"Trust you?" The man laughed. "You come into my home, try to take what's not yours, and think I'm just gonna let you roll outta here?" He released the safety on the gun before turning to the woman. "Get over here."

She shook her head and inched closer to Dro.

"It's okay," Dro soothed before turning his attention to the man pointing a gun to his head.

"Fernando Burman, you're forty-four, you've lived at this residence for the last two years. Before that, you spent most of your time couch surfing at family and friends houses. You don't have a job, at least not one that collects taxes, and you're living off the remains of a convenience store heist from a few weeks ago."

Fernando flinched. "Wait, how'd you—"

"Your mother loved Fernando Llamas. That's who you were named after. Your mother, Shirley, saw the old Nineteen fifty-one classic, *The Lady and the Law*, and fell in love with him. Your father protested but didn't care one way or the other. He was just upset that he had another mouth to feed."

"How do you know that?" the man roared, causing his girlfriend to flinch and inch her way even more behind Dro. It was a move that made him frown.

"I know a lot of things. Like what you had for dinner last night. How many other women you have stashed around town thinking that they're the only one."

This time the woman's face darkened with surprise and then anger.

"I know how much money you still owe Smitty, your drug dealer," Dro continued, "and that your buddy over there on the floor has been pinching money from your hauls."

"What?" He glared down at his still unconscious friend.

"But most important is the fact that I know you don't have a round loaded in the chamber of that gun, and it will take you at least three additional seconds after the original two for being startled, to load it. By then, I'll have pushed your girlfriend out of the way, turned around and disarmed you, and either cocked it and shot you or used it to render you unconscious before calling the police and having you arrested."

The man stared at him in disbelief.

"So what's it going to be, Fernando? Is your lovely lady here worth dying for?"

Seconds later, Fernando slid the gun back into his waistband. "Nah, she ain't."

Lowering his hands, Dro picked up the suitcase, grabbed his client's arm, and left. After helping her into his car, he placed the bag in the trunk. When he shut the door, he winced in pain. Taking a moment, he closed his eyes and tried to focus on breathing. *In and out. In and out.* He repeated it several times. *Jai's right, I'm getting too old for this.*

He waited until he'd driven off before he connected his Bluetooth device and called the police.

* * *

Dro kept up constant chatter for the forty-five-minute drive from Gary, Indiana, back to Chicago. When his client asked to stop and use the restroom, he agreed, assuring her that she was safe and that there wasn't anywhere she could run. Knowing all the signs of an abused woman, he understood that she might feel compelled not to believe that she was safe, and even to contemplate trying to get back to her abusive boyfriend. Despite the fact the man threated to kill her. By the time she left the Ladies' room, he had bought her something to drink and a few snacks.

He drove her straight to Reno's shelter. He'd called ahead, so when they pulled up, Reno and Skyler, his right hand, were waiting at the door. They escorted her inside while he retrieved her suitcase. When he arrived at the reception desk, his client was gone.

"She's back with an intake specialist," Reno confirmed.

He handed Reno her bag and a folder. "Here's my report. It's everything you'll need. Her mother was extremely anxious to hear a word, so—"

"No problem. We'll call her once our new guest gets settled. Thanks, and don't worry, Dro. She'll be safe here."

"I know," he replied, smiling at his brother.

"Dude, you should get to the hospital. You look like crap."

Smiling as much as he could with a sore jaw and busted lip, he said, "I hear the ladies love a man who can hold his own in a fight."

Reno snickered. "That's hardly how it appears. From my *vantage point*, it seems you barely escaped with your life."

"Ah, I see what you did there," Dro shot back, grinning at the subtle reference at his company's name.

"Matter-of-fact, you should've activated that tracking beacon from Daron. By the looks of it, you could've benefitted from an extraction."

"Ha, ha," he said dryly.

"All jokes aside," Reno said, his tone grew serious. "Thank you for what you've done, Dro. I know you just saved this young lady's life."

He shrugged off his friend's praise. "It's what we do." Patting Reno on the back, he turned and slowly headed for the door.

"You going to the hospital?"

"No."

"To see Jai?"

"Uh-uh."

"Then where?"

"Goodnight, Reno."

# CHAPTER 11

"It's a Saturday night. You're really going to spend it cuddled up with a Sherpa blanket, binge-watching TV shows with a bowl of cereal?"

"For your information, I don't have cereal—yet," she snickered.

Lola was sitting on the couch in a pair of pajama pants and a long-sleeved top. She'd returned from the gym an hour prior and after a shower and change of clothes, hadn't moved from her spot.

Her mom had called, and when she found out her daughter was home alone, she began rolling down the list of eligible bachelors she knew in Chicago.

"You don't know them, Mom."

"True, but Ethel told me at our last Spades game that her nephew was newly single. He's not even a mile from your place, and he's a stock trader."

Unable to help herself, Lola asked, "That's only one. Where's the rest?"

"Honey, I wasn't about to rattle them off if you weren't interested," Maggie reasoned.

That made Lola smile. Her mother knew her well.

"Are you still here?" Michelle hedged.

"Yes, sorry. What were we talking about?"

"How you've been spending your raggedy weekends lately."

"Michelle, don't act like you aren't doing the same thing."

"That's lame," Michelle teased. "And I have a date."

"You know, I don't think going out with your brother and sister-in-law counts as a date."

"It does when they're bringing Doctor Davis along."

Lola sat up. "Who's Doctor Davis?"

"Exactly," Michelle squealed with delight. "He works at the hospital with my brother. I hear he's tall, great looking, and if his bedside manner is as sexy as his voice, girl, I'm going to offer him up for prayer at church on Sunday because I might have something to repent from Saturday."

Laughing, she got comfortable while her friend recounted her phone calls with the good doctor.

When the doorbell rang, she slid off the couch while continuing her phone call.

"Who's that? Takeout delivery?"

"Uh, no, I haven't even ordered, yet, thank you."

She gazed out the peephole and almost dropped her phone.

"Michelle, I have to call you back."

"Not 'til you tell me who's at the door. Were you expecting anyone? Do I need to come over there with my taser?"

"No, I'm not. No, you don't, and I'll call you later."

"Wait. Lola—"

"It's fine. I'll call you back."

She ended the call before opening the door to find Dro on the other side.

They both stood on opposite sides, transfixed.

"Hi."

"Hi," she finally managed to say. After the initial shock of seeing him, her gaze traveled past his eyes. She gasped. "Dro, what happened? Were you in a car accident? My God, you look horrible."

She grabbed him by the arm and helped him inside. He tensed at the motion causing her to loosen her grip. When she opened her hand, she saw blood. "Dro, you're bleeding. Did you get cut in the accident?" she frantically asked.

"It wasn't an accident," he replied, his voice holding a weariness she'd never heard from him before. "Someone tried to shoot me. Probably just a graze. It's not a big deal. I'm fine."

"You most certainly are not fine," she determined. "And I don't know where you come from, but not even in Chicago is a gunshot wound just *no big deal*."

Guiding him to the couch, she sat Dro down and helped him remove his jacket. The white shirt underneath was saturated with blood.

"This has to come off."

Dro started to unbutton his shirt, but then stopped midway. Lola picked up where he left off. She threw both garments on the hardwood floor and tried to get a good look at his wound.

"We have to clean this up. I can't tell how bad it is."

He rose. "Lead the way." Dro trailed behind her through the bedroom into the bathroom. He perched on the closed toilet seat while she rummaged in the cabinet for supplies. Running to get a clean washcloth, she returned with that and a towel. Lola washed her hands, then opened the first-aid kit. First, she washed the wound, then wiped it carefully with alcohol. His shoulders tensed against the sting.

"Sorry, I'm out of hydrogen peroxide."

She knelt on the floor in front of him to examine the wound. Lola had to make several attempts due to shaky hands. "I don't think it needs stitches, but I'm no expert."

Dro squeezed her shoulder, reassuringly. "You're doing fine." He glanced down and studied his arm. "It doesn't."

Holding a square bandage in place while she wrapped gauze around his arm, he kept his eyes on Lola as she taped it down.

Unable to help herself, her fingers trailed down his bruised jaw and cut lip. When he didn't stop her, she continued exploring the lines of his face.

When Dro grabbed her fingers, she stilled. *Did I go too far?*

Instead of lowering them, he raised her hand slightly to kiss the inside of her palm. Lola's legs almost buckled.

"Do you know what I thought about as that bullet went whizzing by my head?"

Mesmerized, she shook her head.

"My first thought was why was I stupid enough to die without asking you out on a date."

She trembled at the reference. Before she could say a word, Dro eased her onto his lap and wrapped her in his embrace.

Lola wrapped her arms around his neck and held him tight. Her fingers moved through his disheveled hair, down his bare neck, and then across the expanse of his back. His skin was smooth and warm to the touch.

She was stunned. She had no idea that Dro felt this way, or that she would feel as though her world just skidded to a halt hearing him casually mention that he could have died.

A bizarre mix of confusion, joy, fear, and elation coursed through her body. The combination made her feel heady and slightly nauseous.

Dro pulled away to gently grasp her head in his hands to kiss her lips. A simple whisper of a kiss as Lola was careful not to injure his mouth in the process. He nuzzled her neck.

"Do you want Chinese?"

She stared back. "Dro, you show up on my doorstep shot up, ask me out on a date, kiss me, and now you're inquiring about dinner?"

"Aren't you hungry?" he asked.

Lola stopped for a moment, a dazed expression on her face. Her skin grew clammy, and saliva pooled in her mouth. "Uh-uh. I'm gonna throw up."

His hand snaked out, grabbed the wastebasket, and held it over the bathtub. With him sitting on the toilet, Lola hurled herself in the direction of the basket.  She felt him pull her hair back while she emptied the contents of her stomach. Once the wave passed, she slumped down the side of the tub and leaned her back against the cool porcelain.

"You're in shock," he confirmed. "Give it a minute." He filled the small glass on her counter with water and handed it to her. "Sip it slowly."

Nodding, she did as he instructed. Her eyes drifted shut while she waited for the strange feelings to pass. She felt him take the empty cup from her hand and tie the plastic liner and place it off to the side before replacing it with one of the extras she had at the bottom of the can.

"Better?"

"Yes," she admitted. "Thank you."

Lola opened her eyes to find him observing her.

"Do you ever do anything half measure?"

"No. I never have."

Shaking her head, she accepted his help off the floor. She brushed her teeth and rinsed with mouthwash before cleaning up the supplies strewn across the sink. That task completed, she said, "Hang on, I'll be right back."

When she returned, she held out a gray tee shirt. "Since your shirt got destroyed, I figured you'd want a replacement."

"Unless you're tired of seeing me bare-chested," he teased. Dro held it out in front of him. "Samuels Family Reunion?"

She shrugged. "Best I could do on short notice. It's extra-large, so it should fit."

Dro eased it on. "Thank you."

They returned to the living room and Dro sat on the sofa while Lola located the takeout menus. Claiming the spot next to him, she handed over the stack.

"I like the picture of you and your parents on your nightstand," he said as he scanned the Min's Noodle House menu.

"You're going to tell me that the split second you were in my room, you noticed the family pic by my bed? Come on," she joked. "Nobody is that good."

She asked for his selection and then placed their order on the food delivery app on her phone. She tucked her legs under her and settled in next to him. "It'll be about thirty minutes."

"Your room has golden yellow walls," he began. "A white comforter on your queen-size bed, with a sage throw at the foot of it. Six pillows on the bed, two are the color of goldenrod, two sage green, and two white. In addition to your family picture, you have two books, one of them is a Bible, a ceramic bowl, probably to hold jewelry, a lamp,  and two remotes. One for your television, the other for your DVD player. You have five canvas prints on your wall, all of them are floral arrangements, a chaise lounge with a white throw, a mug on the small rattan trunk, probably last night's tea, and your slippers, which you don't often use because you like walking around in your bare feet."

She tucked her feet further under her before saying, "Okay, that's just plain creepy."

"In my profession, it's imperative to remember even the most minute details."

She absorbed that for a moment. "You know everything there is to know about me, but I don't even know your middle name."

"It's Alejandro. My first name is Victor after my father."

"Siblings?"

"Two brothers, Esteban and Raul. My parents, Victor and Valentina, live in San Miguel de Allende, Mexico. My family is into real estate development and architecture."

"Married?" She threw at him.

"No."

"Last girlfriend?"

He smiled. "More than two years ago. I don't have time to date." She started to say something, but he added, "You're the exception."

Lola's grin went supernova and was bright enough to power the room by itself. "But we haven't been out on our first date yet."

Dro picked up a lock of her hair and wove it around his index finger. "We're having it as we speak. So, how's it going?"

"Well," she answered truthfully. They shared another kiss before she asked, "How long have you been in crisis management?"

"All my life."

That gave her pause. "So, you're never *not* solving problems for people?"

"It's a full-time job, Miss Samuels."

"When do you relax? Go on vacation? Enjoy yourself?"

"I'm relaxed and enjoying myself right now."

She playfully nudged his leg. "Me, too. Though this is isn't exactly how I imagined my evening would turn out."

He gave her his full attention. His gaze roamed across her face as though he was committing it to memory. "But it's better than re-runs?"

Now Lola knew how Jess had felt. Her breath even hitched in her throat to prove it. She glanced down at his mouth and had to concentrate hard on not leaning over and kissing him. "Yes," she finally managed to say. "Now that you've stopped bleeding, but I have to ask one question."

"Anything, name it."

"How often do you get shot?"

# CHAPTER 12

Santiago sat poolside, waiting for Victor and Valentina Reyes to return home from shopping. He was working on his laptop when Esteban walked out of the house.

"This is a surprise," Esteban said as he came over and claimed the seat next to his uncle.

"Before you ask, no, I'm not here for money. I'm here visiting Victor."

"Relax, *tío*. I'm not about to bust your chops," he joked. "I figure my baby brother is thorough enough in that respect."

Santiago sat his computer down. "Alejandro has always been exceptional in everything he does."

"Yes, he has. So, how's work?"

"It'll be better once things come through for me."

Esteban nodded. "Alejandro's helping to get Mayhew off your back?"

"Valentina assured me that he would," Santiago replied. "Plus, he didn't say no. If you've all learned nothing else from Victor, it's that family is everything."

"So is power, uncle. If you have that, everything else falls into line."

Santiago got up and flicked his shoes off. Testing the water, he stepped in and waded toward the deep end. "You sound like your *Abuelo*. He used to tell us that saying every night before bed. Your grandfather had all sorts of sage advice."

"But you didn't take it to heart," Esteban shot back.

Santiago frowned. "I've made a few mistakes, but things will be looking up for me soon. I've got a few new deals cooking as we speak."

"A word of caution, uncle. Alejandro isn't as forgiving as *Papá*. If he bails you out, it's only a one-time deal."

Santiago nodded. "That's all I'll need. Everything is under control. He'll get Mayhew in order."

Esteban sat back and closed his eyes. "For your sake, I hope you're right. But if you're not, I have a few projects I'm working on that I think you'd be perfect for."

He perked up. "Really?"

"But if you're in," he leveled a hard look at Santiago. "I need you all in. No mishaps."

"Of course. So what do you have in mind?"

Esteban's cell phone rang. He glanced at the screen, but didn't recognize the number.

"Hello?"

"Hi Esteban, this is Vikkas."

His expression mirrored his surprise at hearing from Khalil's son who was also an international lawyer. "How are you? What's up?"

"Dad needs to speak with you. Is now a good time?"

"Sure. Hang on a minute." He turned to his uncle. "Sorry, but I've got to take this. I'll be around all weekend, so we'll talk later."

Santiago waved his nephew off. He leaned back in the water until he was floating. Feeling lighter than he had in months, he was finally getting back on track, and business projects would be looking up. He didn't doubt that Alejandro would help him get back on his feet. Victor raised his kids with an iron fist, but he also instilled in them the importance of love, family, and honoring commitments. This time, when he got back on top, he'd stay there. Victor and his progeny weren't the only ones to be reckoned with in their family.

Begging and scraping to his brother's youngest boy for a leg up was degrading, but he wouldn't pass up the opportunity given. He needed his nephew to enact his revenge. The moment he was out from under those bogus loans, the first order of the day would be to ruin Alistair Mayhew. He'd make him pay for causing this type of embarrassment and family upset. And if he got dead in the process, so be it.

* * *

Esteban went into his father's office and shut the door. "Sorry about that."

"No problem, my friend," the man said in the calm, steady voice that Esteban always remembered. "How are you?"

"I'm fine, Khalil. How are you?"

"Recovering," he replied with mirth. "I need a favor, Esteban."

"Of course," he said quickly. "How can I be of service?"

"It is something I would prefer to discuss in person. Can you meet me at the Castle?"

"I'd be happy to."

"Bring Santiago. I believe he can help as well."

Esteban thought about that for a moment, wondering what on earth Santiago could have to do with Khalil. As far as he knew, his uncle hated the man for passing him over for that coveted membership of the Castle. "Sure."

"Great. I'll put Vikkas back on to make all the arrangements."

 While he was waiting, Esteban wondered what could have transpired that required his presence instead of Dro's.

* * *

"You've got to be kidding me," Shawn Mayhew dropped into a chair at the Hyde Park Mission Center. "Can't someone else do that?"

For the third time that morning, Dro had to listen to the young man complain about the assignments he had to complete. Shawn hadn't completed one task yet, and he was already asking to call it a day. The young man was so obnoxious that even the director had voiced regret at accepting Dro's request for Shawn to volunteer.

Lola glanced over at him as if to say, *I told you so.*

Dro never backed down from bullies, impossible challenges, or promises he'd made. If Shawn didn't work out, that would make keeping tabs on Alistair problematic. And right now gleaning information on Mayhew's whereabouts and the company he kept was more important than his spoiled-brat son and his tantrums.

Normally, he only resorted to violence when he had to, but with this young man, Dro was itching to make an exception. After a quick chat with the director to smooth things over, he escorted their reluctant client into an empty office. Lola joined them.

"Shawn, as a man, what is the most important thing in life?"

"Money?"

"No."

"Women?"

Dro pinched the bridge of his nose. "Your word, Shawn."

"Okay," he countered with a mild shrug.

Glancing at Lola over Mayhew's head, she smiled and blew him a kiss. He frowned.

"At the end of the day, no matter what a man has or doesn't have, his word means more than anything else," Dro concluded. "We gave our word that you would complete the work assigned, and that's what you're going to do. This isn't a Country Club."

"You're telling me," he complained.

"You're going to finish every task. No more complaining, refusing to do anything, or not giving it one hundred percent," Dro stressed. "Are we clear?"

Shawn stood to his full height. "Or what?"

"Your option is this or jail."

"Community service is lame." He threw up his hands in frustration. "Besides, my father knows people in this city and has a whole legal team at my disposal. I'd never spend a second locked up."

"I never said it would be in *this* city—or *this* country. I know people, too."

The color emptied from the young man's face. He stared at Dro for any proof that he was joking. When he received none, he gave a short nod, then hightailed it out of the room.

"Did you mean that?"

He turned to Lola. A small gleam flittered across his face. "Every word."

Laughing, she spun on her heel to leave, but he stopped her. "Thank you for the last few weeks. They have been the highlight of my chaotic life."

"You're the one that got shot," she pointed out with a grin. "If you hadn't, we wouldn't be here."

"Oh, we'd be here," he corrected. "I would have eventually asked you out."

"Well, I'm glad you showed up bedraggled on my doorstep."

Dro made a face. "I never show up anywhere unkempt." He leaned closer, and his voice deepened to a seductive whisper when he asked, "Do you know what I'm thankful for, my lovely Lola?"

Her teeth captured her bottom lip. A move that caused Dro to clasp her around the waist and draw her closer.

"No."

"I'm thankful for everything that occurred after that."

Her face turned scarlet, and she had no response to his admission.

Dro continued. "I loved finding out how your lips taste. It drives me to distraction," he replied as he ran a thumb over her lips. His expression went from mild curiosity to avid fascination. "As does your scent."

Lola shifted restlessly in his arms. "Dro…we're at work."

"I know. Say the word and I'll take you home—I'd love to pick up where we left off. With me getting to know you, every nuance, every line of your body, every spot that makes you squirm with desire."

Lola wiped one damp eyebrow. She couldn't believe she was starting to sweat. She glanced up at Dro. He looked completely at ease. Like he wasn't affected by any of his maneuvers. She'd show him that she could give as good as she got. With a smile, she hatched a plan that she would put into effect later.

"Are we still on for dinner tonight?" she said to change the subject.

He nodded. "Unless you want to skip straight to dessert?"

"I'm open to suggestions," she countered boldly.

"I'll keep that in mind. How about my place?"

Her eyes lit up. "You don't think I'm going to turn down an invitation like that, do you?"

His eyebrows drew in. "Are you saying you'd have preferred less dining out?"

"Dro, we've been to dinner practically every night for the last two weeks," she snaked her arms around his neck. "You don't have to keep wining and dining me at expensive restaurants. I'm perfectly happy to eat at home. No-fuss needed. Paper plates are fine."

He held her in a firm embrace. "Are you insinuating that I can't cook?"

"I'm doing nothing of the kind," she clarified with a grin. "I'm merely saying that if you can't, we'll make due."

He reached out and gathered her up in a tight embrace burying his face in her neck. "I don't own paper plates, and I assure you that I can wow you in the kitchen."

"And every other room."

Lola froze in his arms when he lifted his head and burst out laughing.

Her cheeks reddened. "Did I just say that aloud?"

"Yes, you did."

# CHAPTER 13

"Oh no, you don't." Dro backed her up against the nearest wall. He eyed her with very carnal intent. They're playful banter and innuendoes charged the room with sexual tension.

"Don't try to douse it in milk now. That was a deliciously spicy comment, Miss Samuels."

Lola tried to shimmy out of his arms, but his grasp was iron tight. "No, it wasn't."

He bent down, blew his warm breath across her neck, then kissed it. "Your pulse has quickened."

"That's because you're cutting off my air supply."

His fingers traced a path down her jawline and rested on her chest above her heart. "Your skin is flushed and warm to my touch."

"I could be about to pass out from lack of oxygen."

He stared into her eyes. "Your pupils are dilated."

"That's because you're two inches in front of me. Anybody's eyes would be at this close range."

He placed a thumb at the tip of her chin to keep her there before he eased it across her bottom lip. They were a handful of inches separating them from chest to legs. Dro's breath mingled with hers first before he permitted himself the delicious luxury of claiming her mouth. A soft whimper escaped her lips.

Dro pulled away moments later, and Lola closed the distance again.

"You haven't let me go," he growled against her lips. "That sweetheart is the biggest tell of all."

She would have a frank conversation with her body when she got home. It couldn't keep betraying her like this. "I guess you got me," she confessed in a warm whisper.

"Sí, mi Reina."

Her smile was radiant. "I don't know what that means, but I loved the sound of it."

"It means, yes, my queen."

"Uh, excuse me?"

With reluctance, they both turned around to find Shawn hovering just inside the door.

Lola eased out of his arms, but Dro kept his hand at her waist. "Yes, Shawn?"

"I just wanted to say that I'm done. What's my next assignment?"

Dro winked at her. "Progress."

"Progress," she replied. She turned to leave for her meeting with Alistair, but he stopped her.

"Dinner is at 8 o'clock."

"I'll be there. Can I bring anything?"

He bent in and whispered for her ears only, "Just your beautiful smile, and that delectable body of yours."

An hour later, Lola was in Alistair's office listening to him discuss the new building he'd acquired and the need for a media campaign to help promote it after its remodel. Lola took copious notes, but then her mind drifted to Dro.

Remaining professional around him was becoming problematic. Their makeout session earlier proved her point. Meticulous to a fault, she wouldn't have been caught dead making out with her boyfriend at her place of business.

*Your boyfriend.* Her insides turned to Jell-O. How could she help it? In less than three weeks, her life had turned upside down. And everything was sweeter and more alive. There were still some aspects of Dro's job that she didn't know. She also wondered about his affiliation with The Castle, and why he'd suddenly get up to take a call while in a meeting. But in the grand scheme of things, none of that mattered. He made her laugh, she enjoyed his company, loved his sense of humor, and had the highest regard for his professional ability. Victor Alejandro Reyes was the entire package. He hadn't met her parents yet, or she his, but they'd get to that.

What drove her to distraction was that it was getting hard for her to tamp down her desire to pole-vault their relationship to the next level. Wanting to make love to Dro was consuming her days and nights. So far, they had kept things chaste, but it was getting harder to end their evenings with just heaving kissing and hand-holding.

"Lola, did you hear me?"

She glanced up to find Alistair studying her from his desk.

"I apologize, Mr. Mayhew. What was that?"

He shot her a glance from above his reading glasses. His bushy eyebrows furrowed at having to repeat himself. "I asked how things are going with Reyes? I have to admit I was skeptical about the plan you had for Shawn, but it appears to be working."

"It is," she assured him with a wide grin. "Dro has come up with several opportunities for him to give back, in age-appropriate ways."

"His expression darkened. "Dro? You're on a nickname basis already?"

"Yes, we are."

"Uh-huh," he said dismissively. "So, Shawn hasn't been to any nightclubs since this all began?"

"No, sir. Nor has he been hanging around his usual group." She stood, handing him her notes on Shawn's progress. "The press has left him alone for now. As long as he continues what he's doing, there's no reason to think that he won't stay out of the spotlight. In a negative way, of course."

She paused to see how he'd take her comment. She relaxed a bit when he didn't show any sign of being offended.

He nodded. "Great. I guess you'll be able to wrap things up with Reyes soon and be on to other projects?" He walked across the large room, retrieved a folder from the coffee table before settling on the couch.

Lola walked over and sat in the chair closest to it. When she sat down, she had to shift twice before she got comfortable. Her boss's office looked like it was straight out of the pages of Hound and Hearth magazine. She had to hide the smile creeping up her face at her fictional name. She'd joked before that the only thing contemporary in Alistair's office was the view. His private domain was a true representation of his British ancestry. A worn cigar-hued leather sofa, wood-paneled walls, and a hunting theme décor boasted of masculinity, and British ambiance.

Alistair handed her the report before settling back against the cushions. "I'll need you up to speed on this by the end of the week."

The thought of not working with Dro made her stomach tighten. Lola shifted in her chair while trying not to let her disappointment show. "Of course."

Alistair leaned forward, his gaze intent as he asked, "Has he ever told you anything about his work at the Castle?"

Her eyebrows furrowed together. "No. Honestly, I don't understand his work there, but it seems like he's very busy with it. He did mention the position being in his family for years."

Alistair's face grew tense. "Yes, he inherited it from his father." He waved his hand through the air dismissively. "I heard they ran into some trouble over there, but that they're working to turn things around." His gaze narrowed on her. "Did he mention how they're doing with that?"

She shook her head. "Mr. Mayhew, if you don't mind me asking, why the sudden interest in the Castle? You've never mentioned it before."

He shrugged in a manner that conveyed indifference but was far from it. Clearing his throat, Alistair made a show of settling back against the sofa cushion. "No reason. Just curious. You should keep your eyes and ears open when it comes to Reyes. I know he's helping my son, but that's because I gave him no other choice."

"What does that mean?"

"It means he'd like nothing better than to make the Mayhews suffer any way he can."

"I don't follow." She shifted in the seat. "Why are you asking all of these questions or bringing up issues between you and Dro?"

His phone rang before he could respond. "Excuse me a moment."

After speaking to his assistant, he placed the call on hold. When he spun around in his chair, a few things from his desk fell to the floor. Lola came over to help recover them.

"Thanks, but I've got it."

Retrieving the items from the floor, he put a few in his top drawer before coming around his desk. Reaching out, he patted Lola on the back. "I'm sorry I have to take this call."

"Oh, sure. No problem." In truth, she was happy to leave.

"Thanks for working with Shawn," he said, leveling those intense blue eyes on her. "He seems to be less combative at home now and is taking a real interest in what we do here. Honestly, I'd given up on the boy doing anything but spending his inheritance," Alistair confided. "Glad to see he's learning to be more responsible."

Lola blinked a few times at the bizarre shift in topics but decided to go along with it.

"Thank you, Mr. Mayhew. His attitude has improved substantially since he began volunteering in the community. He's coming around."

"Thanks," he said, waving in her general direction.

She closed the lid on her laptop and gathered her things. "Have a good evening, sir," she said and left.

Almost to her office, Lola realized she'd forgotten the report. Turning around, she hurried back to get it. The door was ajar. She raised her hand to knock when she heard him in the middle of a tense conversation over his speakerphone.

"No, I haven't found a way in yet, but I'm working on it."

"Time is running out, Alistair."

"I know that, Lewis," he snapped.

"Thanks to that break-in at the warehouse a few weeks ago, my neck's on the line. And I don't need to tell you that if I go down, you go down."

"Don't threaten me, Lewis," Alistair said through his teeth.

"I don't make threats. I make promises," Lewis shot back. "My sources tell me that they're getting too close, uncovering what needs to stay hidden. We need to step up the pressure to oust them. They're sitting on intellectual property that's worth billions, and they didn't even know it. The medical center—what's in the vault was already slated for deals with foreign governments and labs. Billions, Alistair."

"I get it," he said curtly.

"We need that part of the building back in our control."

"I know, I'm handling it," Alistair said. "The worst thing we can do right now is to get careless."

"I'm not leaving anything to chance. If you don't produce results, I've got someone who will. I'm flying out to meet with him tomorrow."

"Lewis, if you screw this up—"

"I won't. Trust me. After this meeting, we'll have just the insurance policy that we need."

Lola quickly backed away from the door when she heard Alistair slam down the phone receiver. She tried to walk as quickly as she could without drawing attention to herself. *What had she just overheard? Who did he mean?*

She flew into her office and shut the door. Anxious, she paced the carpeted floor. *What did any of this mean?*

Her office phone rang. Absentmindedly, she picked it up. "Lola Samuels, how can I help you?"

"Finally," her mother sighed with relief. "I've been trying to reach you for over an hour. I was worried sick when you didn't return the call."

"I'm sorry, Mom. I was in a meeting and had my phone on vibrate," she answered truthfully. "I just made it back to my desk and haven't had a chance to turn the ringer on. What's up?"

"Wonderful news," Maggie said excitedly. "I was speaking to Jeanie, and—"

Lola sat down at her desk and leaned back in her chair. Norma Jean Anderson was one of her mother's closest friends. She was also notorious around Chicago for being a match-maker. The last thing Lola needed was Ms. Jeanie trying to fix her up.

"Mom," she said, trying to keep her patience on deck. "Thanks, but that's not necessary."

"Oh, did you decide on Ethel's nephew?"

"No." Lola scrunched up her face at the memory of a man who didn't have a clue when it came to manners or chivalry. Pulling out a calculator while on a date to divvy up the bill wasn't her idea of sexy.

"Mom, while I do appreciate all the effort, I don't need a date."

"Why not? Is there a new show out that you've started binge-watching?"

She said it so innocently that Lola knew her mother wasn't trying to throw shade.

"I don't need a date because I already have a boyfriend."

A long pause was followed by her mother's, "Beg pardon?"

She'd tried to rush her mother off the phone, but Maggie Samuels wasn't having it. Lola's ears were still ringing from the barrage of questions her mother had hurled in her direction. The only way she could get off the phone was by promising her mother that she and her father would get to meet Dro soon.

"We'd better," her mother said firmly before agreeing to call her later.

The moment she hung up, her thoughts flew back to Alistair. Two things were certain. Her boss was up to something that sounded very shady, and that he and his associate, Lewis, appeared capable of doing whatever it took to get what they wanted. Even racking up a body count.

# CHAPTER 14

Dro entered the Castle's boardroom room for their emergency meeting. He grabbed two mini sandwiches from the platter, along with bottled water. Sitting in one of the plush leather executive chairs, he downed a sandwich in one bite before turning to Daron.

"What's the topic of this emergency meeting? Are we installing those protective shields?"

Daron shook his head. "It's more serious than that. I need help."

"Name it."

"I need to break into Marquise's mansion," Daron said, sweeping a gaze across the men at the table. " He's got two of my young men in there. This time he's not getting off free and clear."

When Vikkas mentioned that Daron had inherited his Castle seat from a criminal named Bishop, everyone's head turned. Now all the men sat avidly watching the tense exchange between the two men. They went back and forth a few times before Daron pointed out they should be trying to take the criminals down and not throwing shots at each other. All the men agreed and offered their support.

The conversation turned to the Castle and who was responsible for overriding the security system for the attack on Khalil and Vikkas. It was up to Dro to find relevant intel that would lead them to the mastermind behind the attack.

Opening his laptop, he wrote down some notes from their conversation.

Daron pulled up a three-dimensional holographic image of the floorplan of the mansion. Dro studied it. "Am I the only one that thinks his system looks identical to the one at the Castle?

"Yes, but how do we get in? Jai asked.

Daron explained that they'd be wearing suits made of a reflective alloy that allowed the person wearing it to "appear" invisible.

Dro perked up. "Now, that's all types of cool."

Daron introduced the inventor, Calvin, to the group. He explained the practical application for the suits, and how they would get in and out undetected. When the meeting wrapped up, the team moved out.

Once there, Dro turned to Shaz. "Do you know how handy this would've been on a few of my missions?"

"Probably would've saved you from having to take so many butt whoopings," he joked.

"Very funny," Dro shot back. "We can't all sit behind a desk most of the day, counselor. Some of us like to do some actual work."

The two laughed and continued prodding each other until it was time to put their operation in action.

* * *

Lola thought about her meeting with Alistair and his tense conversation. She wondered if she should tell Dro about it, but decide to wait until she could find out more information. The day was back-to-back meetings, so she didn't give her concerns another thought. As she was leaving for the night, Alistair called her into his office. Her stomach hit the floor. *Did he know she'd overheard his call?*

When she arrived at his office, he was shrugging on his coat and preparing to leave.

"Oh, I thought you needed to meet about something."

"No, actually, I wanted to apologize for my behavior earlier. It was horrid of me."

Alistair walked over and gave her a hearty pat on the back. "I truly appreciate all your hard work, Lola. It's been exemplary."

"Thank you," she replied as she followed him out into the hallway.

He shut his door firmly. "Anyway, cheers."

With a wave, he made his way down the hall and out of view. She stood there for a few moments before shaking her head at his strange, abrupt behavior. When she returned to her office, Lola packed up, grabbed her purse and laptop bag and headed out.

She noticed that she'd received a text message from Dro that he'd been called to the Castle for an emergency meeting, but that he'd still meet her for dinner. He just needed to make it later.

*"Would love to."* She texted back.

His reply was immediate. "Great. I'll meet you there as soon as I get free."

She agreed. Now that she had some time to kill, she went to change clothes.

After a shower, Lola stood in her closet, trying to find something to wear. It took a few minutes, but she decided on a pair of jeans and a peach silk, sleeveless blouse.

She brushed her hair and swept it up in a tortoiseshell brown hair clip. She let it naturally fall loosely over the clip with a few wisps framing her face. She re-applied a light makeup and finished with her favorite glossy, peach lip balm. The result gave her a sun-kissed look. Before leaving her house, her cell phone rang. Glancing at the screen, her parent's number.

"Oh no," she said aloud. If she answered the call after dropping the boyfriend bombshell, she would never get off the phone. She dropped her cell into her purse and promised herself that she'd call her mother back before bed.

# CHAPTER 15

Lola was surprised to discover that Dro's house was less than ten minutes from her apartment on South Lake Shore Drive. As she drove along South Lake Shore Drive to East 57th Street, she switched on her wireless headset to call Michelle. Lola told her about the run-in with her boss the day before, and his weird line of questioning about Dro.

"Be careful, Lola," Michelle warned. "Things with Dro seem to be moving pretty fast."

"I know, but is that a bad thing?"

"You tell me. He's loaded, gorgeous, and every woman wants him for her very own. Yet he's single. There's gotta be something wrong with that."

"Or me, you mean?"

"No, I'm not saying that at all," she backpedaled after an awkward pause.

"Really? Because that's kind of what it sounded like," Lola said, her tone was as sour as she felt. She turned onto South Hyde Park Boulevard.

"You know that's not what I mean," her friend clarified. "It's just obvious the man's a workaholic. You've been in that boat before. Two boyfriends ago, Tony used to always put his job before you."

"It was Larry, and it's not the same," she protested, sliding into the left lane. "To start, Dro's boat is a yacht," she joked.

"Not surprising, but I wouldn't be your friend if I didn't caution you to be careful."

"Did you follow that advice with Doctor Davis?"

Michelle chuckled. "So, not the same."

"Seriously?" Lola sputtered. "We haven't known either guy that long, so I fail to see how it's that different?"

After a few false starts, her friend gave up. "You got me. I'll shut up now, but promise me you'll watch your back."

"I always do."

* * *

When Lola pulled up to the curb in front of Dro's house, her mouth formed an o-shape. She'd expected high-end, but this exceeded her expectation. The place was a three-story greystone that appeared to take up almost the entire block. It was the most common type of residential building in Chicago and referred to the grey limestone façade dating back to the eighteen hundreds. She noted that Dro's home was not too far from the Frederick C. Robie house designed by Frank Lloyd Wright. She loved some of his quaint bungalows. The wide variety of architectural gems was just another reason why Chicago had captured her heart.

Turning her attention back to Dro's house, she saw that a row of evergreen trees engulfed the entire first floor of the detached townhome in privacy. She got out of the car and walked up to the gated entryway. She pressed the button and waited. When a man with a British accent said hello, she announced herself and was buzzed into the gate.

Following the concrete walkway up to the house, Lola took a moment to appreciate the large, French double door in rich mahogany wood. The glass was glazed and had an intricate wrought-iron design. Shaking her head, she had to laugh. *And this was just the outside*.

The door opened before she even rang the bell. She gazed up at a tall, handsome, and impeccably dressed man on the other side. *He's British*. Lola reminded herself. So his stylish attire was not surprising. Alistair was also a well-dressed man.

He was wearing navy blue trousers, with a blue striped button-down shirt.

"Good evening, Miss Samuels. My name is Nicholas Travers."

"Nice to meet you," she said warmly before extending her hand.

"Mr. Reyes is in his office and requested that you make yourself at home. He'll join you shortly."

She set her purse on the table just inside the door. "Thank you."

Travers offered her some refreshments, but she declined. "I'll wait for Dro, thank you."

Lola took herself on a tour of the first floor. She would've liked Dro to be her guide, but enjoyed exploring his home just the same.

Dro's place was a pleasant mix of masculine and Mexican beauty.

Touches of his heritage were everywhere. The kitchen, living room, dining room, and music room were all simplistic, yet high-end elegance. But her favorite room was the family room. Rich caramel-colored leather couches flanked a large stone fireplace. There was a pool table with benches along the wall where people could sit and wait for their turn. There was also a holder for the pool sticks mounted on the wall. Across the room was a table with four chairs. Lola could imagine him having friends and family getting together for a card or board game. The entire space felt friendly and warm. The home was a direct reflection of the man.

A built-in bookshelf was next to the fireplace with rows of family pictures. It summoned her like a beacon. She picked up a frame and studied the older couple smiling back at her. *These have to be his parents.* Dro was a blend of both but favored his mother more.

There was a picture of him with two men that she assumed were his brothers. The resemblance was just as strong, except one brother was a few inches taller, while the other was shorter. The shorter one had sandy brown hair and hazel eyes, while the other one had hair as black as Dro's with dark eyes and the same dimples. Both brothers were a bit heavier.

She was taking a gander at his book collection when a loud beeping pierced the silence. It reminded her of a microwave timer that had just gone off, except that no one stopped it. She was about to turn around when a man yelled, "Freeze. Put your hands in the air, and don't move."

Before she could comply, another man grabbed her hands and spun her around. He none-too-gently forced her on the floor on her knees. Seconds later, her hands were bound in zip ties behind her back.

"What is going on," she demanded. "I demand you release me right now."

Not responding, the first man ran a hand-held device over her entire body.

"Where is it?"

"Where's what?" she cried. "I don't know what you're talking about."

"Gray, stand down," Dro roared from the entryway. He ran over and physically pushed the man hovering over Lola aside. "What are you doing?"

He went to step around Gray, but he remained immobile. "We have a code fifty, sir."

"Move aside," Dro warned.

"I can't do that, sir. Not until we've isolated the threat."

Dro opened his mouth to protest, but Gray whispered something in his ear.

Lola watched as his expression rapidly shifted from anger to shocked surprise. When their eyes connected across the expanse, she tried not to show her fear.

"Turn that alarm off," Dro snapped at another man hovering just inside the door.

Gray waved a device around her body.

"Dro?" she said worriedly.

"Hang on, *amora.*"

His security guy motioned to her back around her shoulder blade.

"She's my guest and my girlfriend. Take the ties off."

"But sir—"

"Do it."

The first guy cut Lola loose. Seconds later, she was on her feet with Dro's hand wrapped in hers and him striding for the door. He was walking very fast, making it difficult to keep up.

"Dro?"

He said, "In a minute," but didn't slow down.

When they made it to his bedroom, he shut the door and entered a code on the keypad on the wall. It beeped three times and then went silent. When it did, he turned around and said, "Take off your clothes."

"What?"

"Strip, Lola. There's a bug on you somewhere." He walked past her and into his closet. When he returned, he was carrying a pair of navy blue sweatpants and a matching top. He handed them to her.

"Are you serious?"

"Yes," he replied. He went to the bathroom, turned the light on, and returned to her side. "You can change in there. There's a laundry bag in the linen closet. Leave your clothes in there. I'll need everything," he stressed.

Her hands were shaking, but she quickly discarded her garments and dropped them in the bag. She shrugged into the clothes Dro provided and returned.

"Is this everything?"

"Yes," she retorted impatiently. "Now, tell me what's going on."

He went back to the keypad, entered another code, and the panel beeped again. He opened his bedroom door. Lola was shocked to see two men waiting on the other side.

"Here, get these *cleaned*," was all he said before closing the door again and repeating the security process.

"What does that do?" she asked.

"Secures the room. No one can hear what we're saying."

"Where were you before you came here?"

She frowned. "I was at work. Dro, I meant it. Tell me what the heck is going on."

"I'll kill him for using you this way," he roared.

"Who?"

Striding to his nightstand, he picked up the phone and angrily dialed a number. When the call was answered, he said, "Put a team on Alistair. I want to know where he goes, what he eats, who he speaks to, and what they're talking about—and sweep Ms. Samuel's apartment, too. I'll text you the address."

"Alistair?" Lola breathed.

After hanging up the receiver, he turned to face her. There was an expression on his face and an edge to him that she'd never seen. It gave her pause. "Dro?" she said with concern.

"He placed a bug on you somewhere. My men will make sure he gets nothing."

"Are you kidding me," she snapped. I don't understand. Why would he do that?"

"When you were with him earlier, what did you discuss?"

"He's been a royal pain lately, and now I find out he's trying to snoop on my conversations? I'll bring him up on charges for a hostile work environment and—"

"Lola," he interrupted. "I need you to focus for just a minute. It's important."

She threw up her hands in frustration. "Easy for you to say. Clearly, this sort of thing happens to you all the time. I'm not used to people invading my privacy, using me as a pawn, or threatening people on the telephone, Dro."

"I understand," he said patiently. "But, I need you to relay everything that happened, sweetheart."

She strode past his bed and went to sit down on the gunmetal gray suede couch across the room. Still angry, she perched right on the edge of the sofa. Frown lines still creasing her face. Taking a few moments to calm down, she repeated a breathing exercise to help relax. Placing her hands in her lap, Lola recounted her conversation with Alistair. She mentioned the questions he'd posed about the Castle, and then filled him in on the conversation she'd overheard. That seemed to make Dro even angrier.

"What did you tell him?"

"What do you mean?" She responded, taking in his rigid stance and the anger flashing in his eyes. His tense vibe caused a similar reaction. "I don't think I like your tone. I didn't tell him anything because that's all I know," she snapped.

"He wouldn't answer me when I asked what this vendetta is between your families."

"That's irrelevant right now," he dismissed.

That did it. Lola rushed over and got in his face. "It's very relevant. Look, I want some answers of my own. Like why your invisible security team showed up out of nowhere and pushed me to the ground. If you think I enjoyed being shoved around like I stole something, you're dead wrong. And now you're interrogating me about my boss—"

"That's not what I'm—"

"I'm not a fool," she yelled. "So don't think I'm going to stand here and let you treat me like one. Now, what's going on?"

With his fists clenched at his side, he remained tightlipped, and his expression unreadable.

"You'd better answer me, Dro, and I mean right now."

# CHAPTER 16

"This is going to take a while, and you haven't eaten. Dinner is kind of ruined, but I can get you something from the kitchen, or order in?"

"I don't want anything, but answers," she hissed.

As if to negate her claim, her stomach rumbled.

Tilting his head to the side, Dro waited.

"Fine," she grumbled. "Do you have peanut butter and jelly?"

His eyebrows furrowed together. "Are you sure I can't get you a burger, pasta, or something more substantial than a sandwich loaded with sugar and carbs?"

"It's one of my go-to snacks when people start plucking my nerves." She stared at him for effect.

The right side of his mouth curled up in a half-smile. "I'll be right back."

She watched him go through the security protocol *again* before leaving. It annoyed her all over *again*.

When he returned, minutes later, he was carrying a platter. He brought it to the coffee table and set it down.

She eyed the platter while he secured the room. There were two peanut butter and jelly sandwiches—one on thick wheat bread, the other on white.

"I see you had sugar, *and* carbs."

"What can I say? Nick has a sweet tooth."

Dro also brought two bags of Kettle chips, an apple, a plate of chocolate chip cookies, a glass of milk, and bottled water.

"I wasn't sure if you wanted anything to go with your sandwich," he explained as though she'd asked the question.

While she ate, Dro sat Lola down and explained what the Castle was, and the background of Khalil, his son, Vikkas, and The Kings of the Castle.

"Our mentor stepped down and left the daily operations to what he thought were the capable hands of the managing members. That turned out to be a mistake."

"So, these men Khalil trusted were corrupt," Lola surmised. "And they tried to run the Castle into the ground."

He nodded. "That's the short version, yes."

"What's the long one?"

When he was slow to answer, she said, "Don't try to cherry-pick words now, Dro."

"That's not what I'm doing. There are still men who want to take the Castle back. Khalil showed up with plans to bring us in to restore order, and the next thing we know, he's been shot."

Lola stood and began pacing, the bag of chips in her hands. "But what's their motivation to want it so badly that they'd kill for it?" she queried between bites. "If the members are as corrupt as you say, aren't there plenty of other businesses they could take over. What makes the Castle so special?"

"Because our reach is global and extends from people who are invisible to Presidents, Royalty, and people in power that are governing cities, principalities, and countries. Those numbers have only increased since Khalil founded it."

Lola shook her head. "That much power in the hands of evil would destroy everything and anyone in its wake."

"Exactly," he agreed. "My brothers and I are determined not to let that happen. We've pledged our lives to keep the Castle, the women we love, and each other safe."

Lola digested the information he'd given her. Her mind raced in multiple directions at once. Suddenly, her head snapped up. The whiplash pain that followed made her grimace. "Wait, what does this have to do with Alistair, and why would he put a listening device on me?"

"To get to me," he admitted. "He's had it in for my family since the first time he tried to get my father to do his bidding, and he refused. Since then, he's wanted nothing more than to take our seat at the Castle, but that's not how it works. He'll never get it because it will remain in our family for life."

Lola pondered Dro's justification. "Then why is he going through all this just to keep tabs on you?"

"He wants to know where the Kings will strike next," Dro folded his arms across his chest. "My instincts tell me that Alistair may know who's trying to usurp Khalil's wishes. He may not be the top rung on the ladder, but he might lead us to the players. My guys are still monitoring his calls. I'll have them locate the transcript on the conversation that you overheard. It may provide more pieces of the puzzle."

Leaning against the built-in bookcase, Lola expressed bewilderment. "This is all too mind-blowing, Dro. You expect me to believe that my boss is part of some criminal network that's trying to take over the world as we know it? I've known him for three years, and not once have I seen anything remotely like what you've just described."

Dro shook his head. "World domination may be a bit too lofty a goal for Alistair. Maybe something on the local level."

"This isn't funny," she countered. "Why would he do something like this? Or try and put me under surveillance."

"Like I said, to get to me. He's hoping that our relationship provides him intel he can use to further his cause, but we're on to Mayhew, and have been for a while. He's not getting anything that I don't want him to know. As far as he's concerned, it's business as usual."

"Hang on, you expect me to go in there and act like I don't know he placed a bug on me, that he's invading my privacy trying to get dirt on you, and the rest of the Kings?"

"Yes. You have to. We can't tip our hand."

"I can't do that. The moment I see Alistair I'm going to want to confront him about all this."

Dro's expression turned serious. You can't, Lola. He has to think that all is going according to plan. I know it's a lot to ask of you, but we need you to do this."

Lola continued her pacing, but then stopped short. She sent an accusatory glance in Dro's direction. "It worked both ways, didn't it?"

"I don't follow you."

"Yes, you do," she snapped. "Alistair was trying to pump me for information, and you were doing the same, weren't you, Dro?"

"No, I wasn't."

"But you planned to, didn't you?"

His gaze remained on her.

"If there ever came a time that you didn't have all the dirt on my boss, you were planning to use me to fill in the gaps," she accused.

He moved to her side, his expression resolute. "Yes, I was, but I didn't."

She tried to push past him. "I'm going home."

Dro grabbed her arm. "You can't. It's too dangerous."

"You can't stop me," she retorted, yanking out of his reach. "I'm done playing the pawn in your chess game with Alistair. There's not a bit of difference between the two of you. You were both willing to use me to get what you want."

"Lola, listen to me." He placed both hands on her arms to hold her there. "It's not safe for you to go home, yet. I need to have my men sweep your apartment to make sure it's not bugged, and that no one is waiting for you to return."

"I don't need a babysitter," she dismissed. "I can take care of myself."

"This isn't a game, Lola," he snapped. "These are real-life bad guys, not just petty thieves or men dabbling in corporate espionage." He released her and backed up. "These guys belong to crime syndicates, participate in drug trafficking and the human sex slave trade. They exploit women and children every minute of the day. They have agencies that sell them off to the highest bidder for clients that would gladly pay whatever price required to claim an innocent for their perverted use."

Lola walked over and sank on the couch. Tears caused by an influx of her emotions welled in her eyes. "I'm not going to lie, Dro, this is a lot to take in. I knew you had a multi-faceted job, but that notion pales in comparison. Your life is like a real-time spy movie."

Dro's jaw clenched before he sighed heavily. "I'm involved up to my eyebrows, Lola, and it doesn't just stop. They don't wake up one morning and decide to do the right thing. What they do—" he let out a harsh breath. "Are actions so heinous that you can't even fathom the depths they would sink to get what they want. They are husbands, fathers, and men that on the surface appear normal and worthy contributors to our society, but in truth, it's a façade."

He walked over and knelt beside her and took her hand. "Lola, I understand you're upset, and that you think I was trying to use you. In the beginning, I thought that's the path I would have to take to catch Alistair."

She flinched but didn't remove her hand.

"But I couldn't, sweetheart, not after we began dating. You can be angry, ignore me, or yell because I deserve it, but you'll have to do it here. I can't risk anything happening to you." He placed a hand on her cheek. "I can't. You are too important to me, Lola."

She stared him in the eye. The tears that she'd held in check rolled down her face at the enormity of what he'd disclosed.

"Okay," was her only response.

Dro let out a breath of relief before engulfing her in his warm embrace. This time when he claimed her lips for a searing kiss, the anxiousness they both felt relayed itself without the need for another word. Dro had meant the kiss to be a quick show of affection, but it turned heated in record time. Somehow, they were half-sitting, half-reclining on the sofa, each drifting their hands over the other. Lola possessively ran her hands through his hair and down his back. She wanted to feel his skin touching hers, but his shirt prevented intimate contact.

The moment his roaming hand came in contact with the smooth skin of her stomach, Dro stilled. Reluctantly, he tore himself away and sat up.

"I'm sorry. That got out of hand."

"Don't apologize, Dro." She pulled her borrowed sweatshirt down her stomach. "I'm hardly complaining. I loved it."

"Lola," he said in a voice that echoed his barely-there control.

"Fine," she gave him a playful shove before reaching past him to grab a cookie. "This is very good. Did Travers make them?"

"No, Nick is many things, a baker isn't one of them," he laughed.

They got comfortable on the couch, and instead of watching television, they ended up talking while they polished off the rest of their impromptu dinner. When Lola yawned, he smiled. "That's my cue."

"No, I'm enjoying myself," she murmured sleepily.

"So am I, but it's been a heck of a night, and I think we should get you in bed."

She snuggled closer. "I was fine a minute ago."

"The adrenaline has worn off, and it's been a long day for you."

"Yep," she nodded before glancing up. "Aren't you sleepy?"

"You'd be surprised how little sleep I can survive on."

"Not after tonight," she said dryly.

He smiled before hoisting himself off the couch. "No," she protested the movement. "I was comfortable."

"I think I've got a bed that's way more enticing than my arm."

"Not hardly," she quipped, then laughed. "That was funny."

He reached out, helped her up and into his arms in one graceful movement. "Come on, amora. You can have my bed tonight."

"No," she protested. "I'm not about to take your bed, Dro. I'd be happy to sleep in a guest room." She laid her head on his shoulder. "Looks like you've got fifty."

"I'm not letting you out of my sight," he promised.

Dro lowered Lola's feet to the floor but held on to her as he pulled back the bed covers. As soon as he finished, she crawled into his bed. She got comfortable while he pulled the covers up to her neck.

"Oh," she sighed happily. "I was so wrong. This bed is more comfortable than you."

He chuckled at that. "Told you."

"I should quit," she yawned. "I'm not working for some grouchy tyrant that abuses my trust and invades my privacy."

"You can quit if that's what you want, but we have an opportunity to feed him intel that we decide. We should stick to the plan."

Lola pursed her lips. "I still wanna punch him in the face."

"That would be great to watch," Dro agreed, before leaning down and lightly kissing her lips. He retrieved the remote on the nightstand and pressed a button to dim the lights.

"Buenos Noches, Lola."

She repeated what he said in Spanish and not English. That caused Dro to grin.

"And Dro?"

"Yes, baby?"

"I'm still mad at you."

"I know." He waited until she was asleep before turning on his heel and leaving. At the keypad, he turned off the sound so that she wouldn't be disturbed. "Sweet dreams, *Reina*."

# CHAPTER 17

Dro spoke to one of the men guarding his bedroom before taking the steps to his third-floor office two at a time.

He glanced down at his watch before picking up the phone and dialing a number.

"Hi Alexa," he said when the call connected.

"Hey, Dro. It's been a while," Alexa replied. "How are you?"

He got to the point. "I need your help."

"Name it."

"My girlfriend, Lola, works for Mayhew. The bastard just planted a bug on her."

"Was she compromised?"

"No, we were here when my team discovered the device."

"What do you need?"

"You. I'm concerned about her safety, Alexa. I could use my men or even Daron's team, but I think she'd fair better with you by her side. At least until we figure out Mayhew's endgame."

"Wise move. I'm returning from Seattle tonight. I'll see you in the morning."

"Thanks, Alexa. I owe you one."

"You owe me plenty, she answered. "But, this is free of charge, my friend."

When he ended the call, he made another one to his parents.

His father picked up on the second ring. "What's the problem?" He said without preamble.

"Hola Papá, there's been an incident."

Because it was faster, Dro switched to Spanish to fill his father in on everything that had happened recently. His father listened without interruption. When Dro finished, he merely said, "What do you need, son?"

"I need you and *Mamá* in a safe place. I need you to take a vacation. I know it's short notice, but some things going on here are making me concerned about the safety of my loved ones. For now, I want you two where you'll be safe."

"Dónde?"

"It's in the Outer Banks. La Dova. It belongs to my friend's Aunt. He and his wife are private investigators. I've spoken with them, and everything is arranged. They'll meet you and *Mamá* there tomorrow, along with a security team. The jet will be in San Miguel tomorrow morning. Travers will escort you to North Carolina."

"Alejandro, we're well protected here."

"Not enough," he persisted. "The Kings are getting close to finding out who put the order out to kill Khalil." He closed his eyes. "Mayhew placed a listening device on Lola today. I don't know what he's up to, but he's getting desperate, which makes him dangerous. If he was bold enough to do it knowing what I'm capable of, I don't put it past him or his associates to try to harm those closest to me."

Silence ensued for several long moments before his father asked, "Who is Lola?"

* * *

A few hours later, Dro stepped through the side entrance of the Castle. By the time he wound his way through the maze and reached the boardroom, his brothers were already in their seats. He'd made sure Lola was sound asleep before he left. He'd left a note on the nightstand in case she woke up before he returned home.

He sat down and pulled up his chair. "Sorry, I'm late."

"This has to be important for you to call an emergency meeting," Vikkas concluded.

"Mayhew planted a bug on Lola," he said right to the point.

A collective murmur of surprise echoed around the room.

"I didn't think he had it in him," Daron replied.

Shaz nodded. "The little weasel must be desperate."

"How'd you find the bug?" Vikkas inquired, leaning forward in his executive chair.

"Countermeasures at the house." He grinned. "He won't hear anything I don't want him to know."

"This could work in our favor," Grant pointed out. "If he doesn't suspect you're on to him—"

Dro's expression darkened. "I'm not using Lola as bait."

"Hear me out—"

"Forget it," he shot back. "Would you use Autumn to bring one of these guys down?"

Grant held up his hands in surrender. "Of course not, I wasn't suggesting you put her in harm's way, Dro. Man, if it wasn't clear before, it is now. You care about Miss Samuels."

When he glanced up, everyone at the table was staring at him intently, each with an amused expression.

"Knock it off," he chided. "We need to figure out our next move before I go with my gut and string Mayhew up by the short hairs."

"Wait a moment," Jai interrupted. "What are short hairs?"

A round of laughter circulated the room before Reno leaned over and enlightened Jai. With a smile, he shook his head and said, "Continue."

Shaz swiveled his chair around to face his friend. "While the visual is humorous, that doesn't get us who we need."

"True, but I'd feel a whole lot better," Dro admitted.

Vikkas interrupted their banter. "What news from Prague, Dro?"

"I was supposed to fly out tonight and meet with my contact. He had a lead on some sensitive information he thought could be useful. He wouldn't risk it getting out in the open, so can't delay. I need to leave first thing in the morning."

Grant glanced at his watch. "That's only a few hours from now."

"That's out of the question, considering what happened tonight," Reno replied.

"We need that data, and the man's already skittish." Dro ran a hand over his jaw. "If I try to reschedule, we could lose him."

Grant leaned back in his chair. "Dro's right."

Shaz turned to his buddy. "Where's Lola now?"

"At my house. I've made arrangements to fly my parents to a secure location. I'll do the same for the Samuels. Everyone will leave tomorrow."

"We'll see to it," Daron interjected, "I'll have my men coordinate with your team."

"I've asked Alexa to come on board. She's detailed to Lola."

Daron's eyebrows shot up into his hairline. "Alexa King?"

Dro stared at him. "I wanted someone that Lola would feel comfortable with, and the only man I want around her twenty-four-seven is me."

"She's in good hands then," Daron replied. "I'll contact her immediately to bring her up to speed and get her whatever she needs. Don't worry, brother. Nothing will happen to her."

He visibly relaxed. "It better not, or I'm coming after you—and Alexa."

"Good luck with that," Shaz said dryly.

"Now that that's settled," Vikkas chimed in. "Where do we all stand with our respective projects?"

The meeting wasn't over for another hour. Dro was exhausted, but he felt better. Lola would have Alexa, the Kings, even the Knights, and every asset at their disposal to keep her safe while he was in Prague, and their parents would be out of harm's way. He'd tell Lola about the arrangements when she woke up.

"Dro? Hang on a minute," Vikkas called out.

"Sure." He headed back in. "What's up?" He asked when he reached Vikkas' side.

"I wanted to say thank you so much for connecting us with Dr. Dash. She's been working with my father's medical team, and the serum she had delivered is helping him tremendously. "He's getting stronger and feeling more like himself."

Dro grinned and slapped Vikkas on the shoulder. "That's amazing news. Thanks for telling me. Marena is a wonderful scientist and doctor. I'm glad I could help out, and that her serum is helping Khalil with recovery."

The two patted each other on the back. He gathered his things to leave. He would deal with Mayhew upon his return. The Kings all had a lot on their plates, but everyone was juggling multiple assignments. Now on top of that, they'd be helping to look after Lola.

Dro glanced around the room. A fierce sense of pride and protectiveness rushed through him. These were his brothers. He'd give his life to save every one of them, and he knew they'd do the same. As he walked to his car, he couldn't help but smile. The news about Khalil warmed his heart. He'd call Marena and personally thank her from the plane.

He called Travers to ask that he bring Lola and his luggage to the airport. When his SUV pulled up to the plane, he got out of his car and met Lola and Travers on the tarmac. He escorted her onto Khalil's jet while Travers handed his bag to the attendant.

"You look terrible," she observed.

"Thanks, I haven't slept. I'll take a nap in-flight."

He'd filled her in on the phone about the arrangements he'd made for their parents. She agreed and promised to contact them as soon as they hung up.

"This isn't at all what I pictured," Lola replied, glancing around the plane.

"Really?"

"No, I'm lying. It's *exactly* how I imagined a private plane would look," she laughed. "Michelle is going to have a conniption."

He smiled. "By all means, the two of you can schedule a girl's week out to wherever you'd like to go."

"Don't think I won't take you up on that."

He slid her into his arms. "After you and I have a getaway, of course."

She beamed. "Fair enough."

They sat on the couch while the flight attendant moved around the cabin. He hauled a protesting Lola onto his lap.

"Dro, we're not alone."

"I don't care who sees me holding you in my arms." To prove the point, Dro kissed her senseless.

"You've got to stop doing that." She settled into his arms. "It's hard to concentrate.

He buried his head in her neck and inhaled. "Do you think it's any easier for me? I'm sorry I have to go on this trip, *Reina*. I'd much rather be at home with you. I promised you a home-cooked meal."

"I'm fine with a raincheck," she assured him. "I'll miss you."

He buried his face in her hair. "I'll miss you too, sweetheart." He leaned over to his briefcase and retrieved a dark blue, rectangle-shaped velvet box.

He set it on her lap.

She glanced at the box and back to him. "Dro, what is this?" she said excitedly.

"You actually have to open it up to see." He laughed.

The top creaked a bit as she opened it. Arranged on the blue velvet insert was a gold necklace with a crown pendant made of gold. Each point on the headpiece was a colored gemstone.

"Alejandro," she breathed.

He frowned. "Uh-oh, am I in trouble? It's been a while since you've used my first name."

She hurled herself in his arms. "This is so beautiful, thank you, baby."

"My pleasure. You deserve a whole lot more."

"I don't need you spending a lot of money on me, Dro."

"I know, but it's something that I love to do, Lola, so you will have to indulge me when I want to pamper you."

She kissed him, and then sat back. "If you say so. And thank you for making arrangements for my parents."

"My pleasure. Our parents will be kept safe. Alexa, Daron, and the Kings will be looking after you."

She bristled. "Why do I need this woman and everyone else watching my every move? It seems like overkill. I'm sure they have got better things to do than to babysit me."

He turned so that they were eye-to-eye. "Lola. You mean everything to me. You and my family—that includes the Kings, are my *only* weaknesses. I can't do what I need to do out in the field if I'm worried about any or all of you being in danger."

She crossed her arms. "I don't need a bodyguard."

"Then, just think of Alexa as a friend that's truly gifted in taking down bad guys."

They shared a laugh before she lifted her hand to his cheek. "Okay. I'll do whatever you need me to."

He kissed her. "Thank you, *Reina*. If you need anything, let Travers know."

"I will," she sniffed.

"Hey," he said, wiping the tears from her cheeks. "What's the matter?"

"You'd better come back to me, Victor Alejandro Reyes."

"I promise I'll be home before you even miss me."

"Not likely," she whispered. "In case you haven't noticed, you kinda fill a room." Her eyes darkened with desire as she skimmed a finger over his lower lip.

Dro opened his mouth and captured her finger between his teeth. "You too, sweetheart. I'd ask you to come with me, but I need to focus on my meeting."

"Are you saying that I'm a distraction?"

She watched as his facial expression grew heated.

"Yes, you are," he confirmed. "A beautiful, sexy, one-of-a-kind distraction."

Travers cleared his throat. "Have a pleasant trip, Sir. I'll be waiting outside whenever you're ready, Miss Samuels."

"Thanks, Travers," they said in unison.

They kissed goodbye—again.

"This is hard," Lola cried.

"Yes, but it makes my welcome back much more interesting," he said with a wink.

She couldn't help but laugh as he followed her to the door. "Goodbye, Dro."

"Adíos, mi amora."

Lola stood in front of the car until Dro's jet had taxied down the runway and took off. She brushed back tears as his plane disappeared from view. Travers held the door as she got back in the car.

Nearby, a man lowered his binoculars. "He's gone."

His partner turned the key in the ignition and started the car. "And now she's fair game."

# CHAPTER 18

"Don't take this the wrong way, but who are you?"

Lola peered from under her glasses to see one of Dro's brothers staring at her from the doorway. She sat the laptop next to her on the couch. *Now, which one was he?*

As if reading her mind, he sauntered over to shake her hand. "I'm Esteban."

"I'm Lola."

He nodded. "My brother has never let a woman stay in his home when he wasn't in town. You can't be a fling, so you must be someone truly special."

"I'd like to think so."

Esteban lowered himself into the chair across from her and stretched his legs. "I guess I should've called first. I didn't know Alejandro was going to be out of town."

"It was a sudden trip, but I spoke with him earlier, and he'll be home in the morning."

Esteban grinned. "Ah, so you're living together? I didn't know my brother had it in him."

"I'm just staying here while he's gone." Not sure if she should be honest about her predicament, she said, "My apartment's getting painted. Dro was kind enough to offer up his place while he was away on business."

"I must say, you're not his usual type. Thank God. They were all starting to blend together." Esteban laughed. "You're a refreshing change of pace."

"Why? Because I'm not Hispanic?"

"No, because you can carry on a conversation without stopping to take a selfie."

She burst out laughing, deciding right then that she enjoyed Esteban's sarcastic sense of humor.

"That's the type of woman your brother was attracted to?"

Esteban shrugged. "As you've probably seen, Alejandro's work takes him all over the world at a moment's notice. That's not conducive to a committed relationship."

Lola pondered his words. Isn't that exactly what they were doing? "I have to admit, his work as the King of Hyde Park seems all-encompassing. He said it was handed down within the family line. If that's the case, why didn't the position go to you when your father retired?"

"It did," he admitted, sitting forward to rest his elbows on his knees. "But I turned it down. I have a family, and there was no way I'd be able to dedicate that kind of time for what I've seen, is a very dangerous job." He frowned. "Plus, that was my father's cause, not mine. For as long as I can remember, he's wanted to be the one to change the world. Alejandro's the one bent on solving everyone else's problems. Well, not me. I want to hold on to my little piece of paradise. I have a great life—I'd like to be alive long enough to enjoy it."

She stared at him. His observation of their father explained a great deal about Dro. It was clear now where he'd developed his strong sense of duty and his motivation to help fix things. She glanced at Esteban. There was a pensive air about him that was far from the lighthearted man she'd met just minutes ago.

Alexa King entered the room. She had arrived after Lola had returned from seeing Dro off at the airport. Lola had tried to be aloof and frosty, but it was impossible. The two of them clicked the moment they'd met.

She didn't know what she expected, but Lola wasn't it. She was at least six feet tall, with dark blonde hair down to her shoulders. To say Alexa was fit was an understatement. Just observing her stance and how she carried herself made Lola secretly vow to return to the gym and kickboxing lessons.

Esteban stood.

"Hi, Alexa."

"Esteban," she said smiling. "It's great to see you."

"Likewise. How's everything?"

"Busy, but I love it."

"Of course you do. Well, I think it's time I called it a night. I'm wiped out from traveling, and I need to check in with my wife and kids."

"Sure," Lola replied, standing. She went over and shook his hand. "It's nice to meet you, Esteban."

"Likewise, Lola. See you in the morning Alexa."

She nodded.

When they were alone, Lola said, "He was acting a little weird. I wonder why that was?"

"He lost an arm-wrestling match with me," Alexa admitted. "Twice."

* * *

That evening, Lola was snuggling under the plush covers in a guestroom she'd picked for herself when Dro called. Gleeful, Lola picked up her cell phone.

"All settled in?"

"Hello to you, too. And yes, I'm very resourceful. I've already picked a bedroom and unpacked."

"Good to hear. Is it mine?"

"No, sir," she drawled. "It's the yellow one. It reminds me of a spa."

"I was going for a relaxed Zen-type thing, so I guess my interior designer knew what she was doing," he joked. "Is Alexa all settled in?"

"Yes, she is. Dro, how long do I need to be here, and have a bodyguard? I can't hide out here forever. I've got work. Besides, won't Alistair suspect something if I stop coming into the office, or I come back with an Amazon in tow?"

"*Reina*, I don't want you anywhere but there while I'm gone. It's the safest place for you to be, Lola."

"As for Alistair, I don't want him thinking his plan isn't working. I want his guard down. He'll get sloppy at some point, and that's when I'll find out what I need to know."

She hoisted herself upwards and got comfortable against the fluffy pillows. "How? You all have the device he placed on me. Won't he get suspicious when it's been hours, and there's been no discussion for him to eavesdrop on?"

"I'm not talking about him hearing us. I'm talking about me surveilling him."

"I don't follow."

"When you took me on a tour of his office, I placed a bug of my own. I've got a team on transcribing everything he says. Eventually, he'll say something worthwhile, and then I'll nail him."

"I'm no lawyer, but I don't think that's evidence you can use in court to bring him down."

He chuckled. "Shaz said the same thing. I'll tell you what I told him. I'm not interested in dragging him into court so that he can get off. At the Castle, we work outside of the confines of normal channels."

She shook her head before burrowing back under the covers. "I've been dropped into the pages of a spy novel."

"Welcome to my world, Lola. It's not for the faint of heart. But know that I will do anything needed to protect you and keep you safe from harm. I know it's more than you signed on for, but—"

She bolted upright. "Are you trying to dump me, Dro?"

"Of course not," he countered with an indignant tone. "What gave you that impression? I'm merely trying to say that I care about you, Lola Samuels. Deeply. But I don't want to assume anything. I want you to decide for yourself if this is all too much for you or not."

Her heart almost beat itself right out of her chest. She was crazy about this man. He always put everyone's feelings and wants before his own.

"You're the biggest boy scout I've ever met, Dro." She laughed. "Yes, I'm here. I'm not going anywhere. And I care about you deeply, too."

There was silence for a moment before he spoke. "Good to hear, *Reina.*"

They continued talking about more lighthearted things like meeting each other's parents and Michelle's progress with Dr. Davis."

"I'll do a quick background check on the good doctor just in case."

"You will do no such thing," she replied trying not to laugh.

"What kind of girlfriend are you? You don't let me have any fun."

She shook her head. "Who investigates people and calls it fun?" Before he could retort, she said, "Oh, I forgot to tell you I met your brother."

"What? Which one?"

"Esteban. He arrived earlier this evening."

"Did he say why?"

"Dro, he needs a reason to visit?"

"Yes," he said, his tone bland. "Esteban has a reason for everything. I'll call him after we get off the phone."

"Okay," Lola replied, during the middle of a yawn.

"Which sounds like right now."

Lola pulled the covers up to her neck. "What time is it where you are?"

"It's four in the morning here in Prague."

She closed her eyes and nestled into the fetal position. "Were you successful?"

"Yes, I was. I'll be home late tonight."

She grinned like someone had given her a dozen roses. "I can't wait to see you."

"Sweetheart, I have to go."

"Be safe, Dro."

"Always, *Reina.*"

# CHAPTER 19

"Your call went well?" His contact inquired in Czech.

"Ano díky, Hajek."

"You're welcome. Your Czech is improving," Mr. Hajek replied with a grin. He pointed to the laptop sitting on the desk. "The money transfer is complete. Thanks, my friend."

"You're welcome. I verified the files were uploaded to my private server."

Mr. Hajek stood. "Then, our business has concluded." He walked around his desk and shook Dro's hand. "Until the next time."

The door behind them burst open, and a man ran in. He spoke so rapidly that Dro couldn't make out what he said.

"We have to go. Quick, this way," Hajek urged, running to another door in the small office.

Dro rushed after him and shut and locked the door behind him. Hajek moved some boxes aside on the back wall. He pressed the wall, and a panel door opened.

"Quick, through here," he said in English.

Dro crouched down and hurried along the hidden path. Hajek closed the door behind them and was quick on Dro's heels. "Make a right up ahead."

"Now next left," he said after they'd traveled about a minute.

Gunshots sounded off in the distance. That hastened their pace.

Arriving at a small entrance, Dro called over his shoulder. "There's a cipher lock on the door."

"2, 7, 8, 5, 9."

Punching the code in, Dro turned the handle and yanked it open. Jumping out feet first, he moved out of the way to make room for Hajek to take the lead.

Once through the exit, they came out in an alley and bolted down the street. Hajek ran into a restaurant and went straight through the kitchen.

"Cerny, auto," he yelled.

A man plucked a set of keys off a corkboard and tossed them at Hajek. Catching them in mid-air without breaking a stride, he headed out the back.

He slid into a black Fiat 500 and unlocked the door. Dro slipped into the passenger seat and buckled up. Hajek was backing up before he'd even closed the door.

Taking his phone out, Dro pounded out a text message.

"Time to go, Dro."

"Way ahead of you," he replied. "Drop me at the airport. They'll be ready when we get there."

* * *

When they arrived, Dro turned to his friend. "Thanks for everything. Will you be okay?"

"Of course. Don't worry about me." Hajek smiled. "I've got countermeasures in place. I know how to become invisible, my friend."

He patted his buddy on the shoulder, jumped out of the car and ran the few feet to the plane. Two men from his team met him at the bottom of the steps.

"We're clear for takeoff, Sir."

"Get us in the air, Gray."

"Roger that."

All three rushed up the steps and into the jet.

While the flight attendant secured the door, Dro took a seat. He eased out of his jacket and tossed it on the seat across from him, followed by his tie. Sitting back, he buckled his seat belt. Now that the adrenaline was ebbing, he stifled a yawn.

Closing his eyes, he attempted to steady his breathing.

"Mr. Reyes, can I get you a drink?"

"A club soda," he replied without opening his eyes. "Thanks, Jan."

"My pleasure, sir."

*You got it.* The list he acquired would provide the Kings with some of the key players involved in trying to take back the Castle and possibly Khalil's shooting. When he got home, he'd share his findings with his brothers.

His thoughts turned to Esteban. It was anyone's guess why he'd turn up without telling him. He'd wanted to spend as much time as he could speaking with Lola, so he decided his brother could wait.

On edge, Lola had occupied his thoughts the entire trip. Though he had complete confidence in his and Daron's teams to be able to protect her, realistically, he'd exhale once he was back home, and she was in his arms.

*Lola.* She was his queen, his *Reina,* and always would be. The more he thought about never letting her go, the calmer he became. When he returned to Chicago, he would ensure that she knew how happy he'd been from the moment they'd had that crazy first date.

His eyes were still closed, but he allowed himself a lazy grin. Yes, Lola had done what no other woman had been able to accomplish. She'd gotten under his skin.

By the time the flight attendant returned with his drink, Dro was sound asleep.

# CHAPTER 20

"I don't want to hear excuses, Miss Samuels. I want solutions. Now either you get in here and fix this mess, or you're fired."

How many times in three weeks could he threaten to fire her? It had been so often it was becoming white noise.

Alistair had hung up the phone before she'd even said goodbye. She was hoping not to have to go into the office, but that hope just got ripped to shreds.

She hurried into her bedroom to get showered and dressed. Lola didn't know where the disconnect was, but her team forgetting everything they'd gone over in their last meeting was unacceptable. Several of the interviews she'd set-up had been canceled, they'd missed a deadline to submit print content for one of Chicago's premier Architectural magazines, and now Alistair was on a rampage. After he was done chewing her out, she'd return the favor to her lax team.

It took some doing, but she'd convinced Dro when she called him back that she needed to go into work. At first, he'd been adamant that she stayed put, but after several minutes of verbal sparring, he agreed.

"Only if you take Alexa with you, and wear the earrings Daron gave you."

"Done," she agreed.

She glanced at the phone. "Dro, I have to go, Alistair is calling back."

"Goodbye, beautiful."

She beamed with delight. "See you later," she replied before clicking over to the second line.

"Hello, Mr. Mayhew. What can I do for you?"

"You can get here thirty-minutes earlier," he snapped. "We need to go over some revisions to the campaign you're doing. I've got an outside meeting, so the sooner, the better."

"Yes, sir," she responded before hanging up.

She shook her head and made a muffled screaming sound as she headed for the bathroom.

* * *

After she'd showered and dried off, she picked out an outfit from her closet. If she was going to have to listen to Alistair's rants, and give some of her own to her team, she wanted to be comfortable.

By the time she dressed, she was running late.

Glancing at her watch again, she pondered calling Alexa. She'd gone over to meet with Daron on some new tech that he wanted her to try. She and Dro had joked about Daron's excitement at getting new devices. They called it, Tech Day.

She wouldn't have time to wait for Alexa to come to her apartment. Lola decided that she would call Alexa when she got to work. With a plan in place, she went to her Jewelry box to retrieve the tracking earrings. Lola decided to carry it from her closet to her vanity table for better light.

Lola was halfway there before she tripped on the towel she'd left on the floor. The large wooden jewelry box crashed to the carpet scattering the contents everywhere.

"Nooooooo, not now," she wailed. She was already late, and this setback wasn't helping.

"I don't have time to sift through all this stuff to find my babysitter earrings," she complained. Putting on a different pair, Lola did wear a ring that Alexa provided. It looked like a normal cocktail ring, but when you turned it to the right, a set of sharp points jutted out, turning the piece of jewelry into a dangerous weapon.

Not only was it used for self-defense, but it could also collect a DNA sample. The user would swipe it along someone's skin, then twist the ring in the opposite direction. The small claws would retract hiding the evidence safely. For now, that was the best she could do.

Grabbing her briefcase, keys, and purse, Lola rushed out the door. Once she'd put on her telephone headset and connected her phone, she called Dro.

While she drove, they made plans for dinner. Lola announced she was cooking. Esteban was still there, and Alexa, so it would be the four of them. Excited, she planned out the menu and what she'd pick up at the grocery store that evening.

"I'll have Travers pick up everything you need," he informed her.

"Dro, part of the fun is doing the shopping," she told him. "I've got this."

"Oh, can I speak with Alexa? I need to ask her something about a file she sent me."

"I'll have to call you back," she said quickly. "Sorry, mom's calling."

After hanging up, she felt very guilty about lying. So much so, she called her mom just so if pressed, Lola could say they spoke.

Her mother spent the entire call gushing about how wonderful La Dova was.

"I know we haven't met Alejandro yet, but honey, his taste is impeccable."

She laughed. "Mom, it's not his resort."

"I know, but still, he's called to check on us, sent flowers, and even arranged dinner with his parents. Oh, wait till you meet them. Valentina and Victor are so wonderful. Great, salt of the Earth people. I've even learned a few words in Spanish. Watch," her mother instructed. "Hugh, *ven aca*. I just told your dad to come here."

"Wow, mom, that was very nice."

"We're having the best time," Maggie sighed. "Oh, Lola, I have to go. Valentina and I are learning how to make sea glass jewelry while the guys go sailing on a catamarin."

"It's a catamaran," Lola corrected.

"Bye, honey, we love you."

* * *

Maggie hung up. "Whew, that was close. I thought I was going to slip up."

"You did well," Valentina replied, patting her hand.

"Normally, when I'm trying to hide something, Lola can tell. The last thing I need is her cross-examining me. I'd spill the beans for sure. If she knew we were actively plotting to move her relationship with Alejandro along, she'd kill me."

"You? What about me? My son is a human lie-detector," Valentina chimed in. "He always tries to plan for and anticipate everything. Even as a little boy he was the same way. Do you know how hard it is to surprise someone that's always on high alert?"

"Oh, I understand. Lola says she isn't big on surprises, but she loves them."

Valentina sipped her Passionfruit Iced Tea. "So, what should we do?"

Silence ensued. Both women's eyebrows were knitted in concentration.

"I got it," Maggie said, triumphantly.

Valentina clasped her hands together with excitement. *"Excelente. What?"*

Maggie beamed. "Let's help plan their wedding?"

Valentina choked on her drink. "Are they engaged?" She groused before switching to rant in Spanish.

"No, no. Lola and Dro aren't engaged," Maggie said quickly. "But why should that stop us? You, Victor, Hugh and I are enjoying each other's company, so why not work to get our children together permanently?"

Valentina squeezed Maggie's hand. "Let's get started."

* * *

Lola had chuckled at her mother, practically hanging up on her. She was glad that her parents and Dro's were getting along.

Chuckling, she decided to check in with Michelle. "Okay, I'm having dinner tonight for Dro, and his brother, Esteban. What should I make?" She said when her friend picked up.

Lola hadn't told her about the need for Alexa. She felt bad about not sharing with her best friend, but Dro had convinced her that the less Michelle knew, the safer she'd be.

"Esteban? Sounds sexy. Is he?"

"Yes, he is good looking," Lola confirmed. "Wait, where's Dr. Davis?"

"Oh, that didn't work out," she replied. "Our good doctor works too much, and when he gets home, he's usually sleeping five-minutes later. His car sees him more than I do."

"I'm sorry," Lola replied. "I know how much you liked him."

"True, but the best way to get over someone is with a new distraction. So, tell me about his brother."

"Not happening. Esteban has a wife and kids."

"Drats," Michelle whined. "Do they have any cousins?"

Lola chuckled. "Of course, they do. I don't know them yet. Look, I've got to run. I just arrived at work."

"Good luck," Michelle replied. "Your man's loaded, so if you feel inclined to quit and tell Mr. Mayhew where he can stuff his job—"

"Uh, not happening. I'm not quitting my job, nor do I have any plans to live off my boyfriend."

"You're boring," Michelle teased. "How am I supposed to live vicariously through you?"

Lola laughed while she maneuvered her car into the parking garage. "You're not. Now go back to work. We'll chat later."

# CHAPTER 21

Lola reclined in her chair with her stockinged feet on the desk. It had taken all day to put out the numerous fires around the office. Satisfied that Alistair was appeased and her projects back on track, she allowed herself a few minutes to relax. When her cell phone rang, she seriously considered not answering it until she saw who it was.

She lowered her feet to the floor. "Hey babe, are you back?"

"Not yet, I'm driving home from the airport. Imagine my surprise to find you *still* at work."

"I know. Alistair asked me to come in early. We had to go over some things before his meeting."

"Lola—"

"I know," she cut him off. "I've heard that absence makes the heart grow fonder."

He sighed. "My heart was pretty fond of you already, but this is serious, Lola. We can't let our guard down. The fact that Alistair is waltzing around acting like business is as usual worries me. When are you getting here?"

"Soon. I have to stop at the—whoa, that's odd."

"What's odd?"

"The lights went out."

"Why? It's not even six o'clock yet. Is it just your office? Try calling maintenance."

She slid out of her chair and stepped into the hallway. She spotted a group of men gathered on the opposite end. They looked like a work crew.

"It's not just my lights," she whispered. "I'm out in the hallway and see workers. It looks like the whole floor."

"Dro," she said suddenly, her voice held a hint of alarm. "Wait, I was wrong."

"About what?"

"They aren't maintenance. They have duffle bags, not toolboxes."

"Lola, what do you mean? Who?"

"Did you send somebody?"

"No, I didn't. Who's there? What do they look like?"

"Dro," she said with concern. "They're coming this way."

"Don't worry. Go back to your office. Alexa will check things out."

Lola scrunched up her face. "She's not here."

"What? Where is she? Why would she leave you?"

"She didn't," Lola explained. "I left her."

"My God, Lola. How could you—"

"We don't have time for a lecture," she whispered. "Dro, they're coming this way."

"Okay," he replied calmly. "Go back into your office and lock your door."

"Dro—"

"Do it, Lola. Get inside and lock the door. Find something to wedge under the doorknob," he said calmly. "A chair works best."

He heard her struggling on his end of the receiver, before she said, "Okay. Done."

"That's great, sweetheart," he said. "Now, I need you to check your office phone and see if you get a dial tone. If you do, call the police. I'm sending Daron a text on my end."

She did as he instructed. "It's dead. Dro." Worry crept into her voice. "Who are these people?"

"I don't know, baby, but I'm on my way. I'll call Alexa and have her meet me there. Lola, I need you to stay on the phone and tell me everything you can about who you saw. Can you do that?"

"Yes."

Her voice shook, and it nearly crushed his heart. "Good," he encouraged while he raced across town. "Now, how many men did you see?"

"I think there were four."

"Okay, what were they wearing?"

"All black. They have vests. Dro, they had helmets on," she replied. I couldn't see their faces."

"Did they have weapons?"

"I don't know, I can't remember," she said in a ragged whisper.

"It's okay," he soothed. "I'm almost there. Lola, I need you to activate your tracking earrings for me, okay?"

There was silence for a few moments.

"Lola, are you still on the line?"

"Yes. Dro, I'm sorry, but I don't have them on. I'm sorry," she repeated when he didn't reply. "I was running late and trying to get here on time. I dropped my jewelry box on the carpet and didn't have time to pick it up," she finished in a rush. Tears began running down her face. "I've really messed up. This is all my fault."

"No, you didn't, *Reina*," he whispered. "It will be okay. I need you to remain calm.

The next thing Dro heard was loud banging.

"Sweetheart, tell me what's going on?"

"Dro, they're trying to knock down the door," she wailed.

He activated the handsfree capability on his phone while trying to weave in and out of traffic, managing to send a code to Daron's phone. He was minutes from Mayhew's building.

"Listen to me, push the desk or any furniture you can move up against the door. Next, find a weapon, Lola. Something heavy that you can use to defend yourself. A lamp, coat rack, whatever you have that you can easily swing. Get behind the door. If they break it down, you slam whatever you have up against the head of whoever comes through that door first. Don't worry, you can do this."

"Okay," she said. He heard her put the phone down. His heart sank.

The next thing he heard made his blood boil. Lola was screaming, followed by the sounds of a scuffle. He heard a man yell, followed by a crash and more yelling.

"Lola?" Dro called out as loud as he could. Then, he heard silence.

# CHAPTER 22

Lola had done exactly what Dro had told her. She pushed every bulky item she could find up against the door before hiding behind it. She didn't have a coat rack, but she did have two lamps, and a telephone console. Yanking the cords out of the wall, Lola sat them on the floor next to her feet. She twisted the ring on her finger to expose the metal claws, grabbed the telephone, then waited in the dark. She kept looking around the room to help her eyes get acclimated to the dark.

It took several attempts, but the lock broke. The first man through the door had to scale the debris in front of the entrance. While he was trying to maneuver, Lola cracked him upside the head with the phone. He slumped unconscious on the mound of furniture.

Effectively, she'd created a bottleneck where they could only come in one at a time. The next man received a hit upside the jaw, while the third took a blow from the lamp. While she moved to receive another lamp, a man jumped over the pile and into the room.

She swung the lamp, but he ducked before knocking it out of her hand. He attempted to grab her, but she slipped away from him. Spotting her purse on the floor, Lola dropped to the floor and tried to crawl across the room.

A man grabbed her leg. Lola spun around and kicked him anywhere she could reach. Her bare feet hurt, but she didn't care. Eventually, he yanked her upright and placed an arm around her neck. Lola didn't panic. Instead, she remembered the moves Alexa instructed her to do.

Placing her arm on her assailant's forearm, she bent down and bit him as hard she as she could before jabbing her elbow into his stomach. Using her hand as a hammer and slamming it into his groin. The man yelled and dropped like a stone.

She used her open palm to slap him across the face. Her ring connected and must have done some damage because he roared in pain.

Lola was about to feel around for another weapon to use when she saw a red line dance across the darkness and inch up her dress. Her eyes flew to the door where she could barely make out a man holding a gun that was aimed right at her chest.

* * *

Dro was the first one to arrive. From the outside, he noticed that only the top floors were without power. He took the elevator up as far as he could then scaled the stairwell. Dro ran up the last few flights of stairs. Opening the door slowly, it took him a few seconds to get acclimated to the dark. He sprinted to Lola's office and through the door. It was empty.

He was so angry, he yelled before picking up a chair and hurling it across the room.

His cell phone rang.

"Yes?" he said woodenly.

"We've got your woman."

Dro spun on his heel and ran for the stairs. He flew down them. "Let me speak to her."

"Sorry," a man said over the line. "She's tied up at the moment."

"Who are you?" Dro snapped. "If you hurt her in any way, I'll kill you."

"Give us what we want, Mr. Reyes, or we start delivering pieces of your girlfriend in gift boxes."

"What do you want?"

"The list you acquired in Prague," he demanded. "You give us that, and we let your little Lola here, live."

"If you know who I am," Dro warned. "Then you know what I'm capable of doing. If you harm her, I'll find you. And when I do, dental records will be the only way anyone will be able to identify your body."

"Time is wasting, Mr. Reyes. Get us what we want."

"I'm not giving you a thing until I confirm that she's alive."

There was a shuffle, and then Lola said, "Dro?"

He closed his eyes. "Lola. Don't worry, *Reina*, I'm coming for you."

"I know."

Her voice was calm, but he could still hear the fear. A red haze drifted over him. He was so angry, he was shaking.

"We'll be in touch with instructions on where to send it." The man returned to the line. "Don't bother trying to track this call or locate our signal. You won't find us."

* * *

"You can't give in to their demands," Grant replied, scanning the faces of the other Kings. "If you do, she's as good as dead."

"What choice does he have?" Reno countered. "If he doesn't, they'll kill her."

"Nobody is harming Lola," Dro said in a voice devoid of emotion. "I'm going to find her."

"*We* are going to find her," Daron remarked, coming into the Castle boardroom with Alexa in tow. He motioned for her to take a seat.

Dro glanced at them. "Anything?"

"Not yet," Alexa admitted.

"I won't lie, Dro. Without the tracking earrings, our progress slows significantly. I'm not saying it's impossible," Daron corrected. "Merely that locating Lola will take time. He sat down in his chair and retrieved numerous folders from his briefcase.

"We don't have time," Dro barked.

"Did the note they sent contain any clues?" Alexa inquired.

Antsy, Dro, paced the boardroom. "No. The analysis showed no fingerprints found or anything that could provide some insight into Lola's whereabouts."

"My team has tapped into the City's database and will review all the traffic camera footage," Daron replied. "But they haven't been able to retrieve the security tapes from Mayhew's company."

"Leave that to me," he told Daron. "I'm sorry I was short earlier. I know I shouldn't be taking this out on you—"

"It's okay, man. I understand."

He turned to Alexa. "Thank you both for working on this. I know neither of you will rest until Lola's home safe."

Alexa and Daron nodded. Dro snatched his jacket off the back of his chair and hurried out of the room.

"Dro, wait a minute."

He spun around and found Jai behind him. "I don't have a minute," he said tersely.

"I'm worried about you," Jai said. "When's the last time you've eaten or slept?"

"I don't know," he answered honestly. "But, I'm fine."

"You're not fine," Jai continued," Placing a hand on his shoulder. "Your woman was kidnapped. Who would be fine under those circumstances? I'm not just your physician, and brother, Dro. I'm your friend. You won't be any good to Lola if you're not in peak form."

Dro ran a hand through his hair. "You're right. I do need to rest and take care of myself. But I'll do it *after* I find her, Jai. What if the tables turned and you were in my place? What if they'd kidnapped Temple instead? Or India? Would you be worried about eating or sleeping until she was safe at your side?"

"You're right, Dro. I would move mountains to bring her back unharmed." Jai clapped him on the back. "Watch your back."

"Always do."

# CHAPTER 23

"Going on a hunger strike won't cause us to let you go."

Lola ignored the man holding a platter at the entryway to the bedroom. She'd done so for the last two nights. She wasn't about to give her captors the impression that she was fine with being abducted, far from it. Lola had messed up big time. Ditching Alexa was bad enough, but not wearing the tracking earrings she'd been given ensured that there was no way for the Kings to find her. Dro's security team might have taken minutes to get there, but because of her disregard for protocol, she was in the arms of the enemy.

They'd covered her head when they kidnapped her, and there were no windows in her room, so she had no point of reference for the time other than her internal clock causing her stomach to rumble when she was hungry or the need for bathroom breaks. Right now, she was ravenous and tired, but she refused to get used to the hospitable treatment. She was a prisoner. She didn't know why she was being held captive, but she knew that she was alive only as long as she was helpful to their cause.

The men used no names, wore masks, and voice modulators so that she couldn't make out a face or a familiar voice.

Lola tried her best to fight off the sense of hopelessness, or feelings of despair. Before she was taken captive, she'd hid her ring in her bra. They hadn't searched her past a pat-down. It was safe. Alexa assured her that if she scratched someone with it, they would be able to get a DNA sample and find the bad guys. Lola was counting on it.

Her saving grace was knowing that Dro would come for her. It may take longer, thanks to her stubbornness, but he would get there. She would stake her life on it.

Then you have to bide time until he finds you. You can't do that starving to death.

"Wait," she called out. "Please leave it."

"Changed your mind, huh? Smart girl," the man chuckled and set the food and water down on the table. His voice sounded like a creepy Chipmunk.

She waited until he left before she attacked the food. Lola tried her best not to wolf it down. She needed her wits about her, and not become doubled over with indigestion. Halfway through the meal, she pondered something. *What if they poisoned it or slipped something into the food?*

A moment of full-blown panic took over before she tamped it down. That wouldn't make sense. She wasn't useful dead. If Dro had already given them what they wanted, she'd be free. The thought of him not negotiating gave her pause.

He'd impressed upon her the seriousness of their work. The nature of it would prohibit him from giving up whatever someone demanded.

That thought caused the food to lodge in her throat. He'd said before he'd be willing to die for their cause. Millions of lives were at stake. How could she expect him to jeopardize all that the Kings were doing to save only one person?

Her fortitude that was barely in place began to slip. *Dro can't save you. He won't.*

Lola shoved the plate of half-eaten food away and trudged back to the small bed. She laid down, eased the coarse blanket around her like a protective cocoon, and gave way to tears of fear, doubt, and uncertainty.

* * *

Alistair unlocked the door of his English Tudor-style manor home and entered. He stepped into the grand foyer and tossed his keys into a large ceramic bowl sitting on the wood table. The place was dark. He tamped down some annoyance at his staff. Not having the entry brightly lit upon his arrival was one of his pet peeves.

Grumbling under his breath, he headed into the Library. Without bothering to turn the light on first, he went straight for his liquor cabinet and poured himself a stiff whiskey.

"I wouldn't do that just yet."

"Bloody hell," Alistair exclaimed before whipping around and peering into the darkness towards the only two chairs in the room.

He heard the click of the lamp, and then the room was flooded in brightness. When he saw who was there, he placed his untouched glass on the bar.

"What are you doing here? How dare you break into my house?"

"Spare me the feigned surprise, Mayhew," Dro growled, loosening his shirt collar as the heat from his body almost became unbearable. "You had to know I'd come. You knew the moment you paid Orlov's men to kidnap Lola that this meeting was inevitable. The problem is…" Dro crossed one leg over the other. "You expected you'd have an army of men here to protect you when it happened."

Alistair's face drained of color, leaving it a gray-tinged white. "Reyes, this is—"

"You don't really want to deny something that I know is true, do you?" He asked, his anger evident, even with the measured tone. "That will only piss me off, Mayhew. And when that happens, I tend to enjoy my work a lot more. Just ask Orlov." A slow smiled drifted across his face. "That may be hard for a few weeks. He'll probably need his jaw wired shut."

"Now see here, I don't know what you think you know, but—"

He didn't have a chance to say another word. Dro flew across the room and grabbed him by the scruff of his neck. He'd slammed Alistair in a chair and had his hands tied behind his back before the older man had a chance to recover.

"Where is she?"

"I don't know—"

The first blow caused Alistair's head to snap back. His legs flew out in front of him in an attempt to shove his chair backward. The second caused blood to trickle down his nose.

"Stop, stop. Think about what you're doing," he whined.

"Oh, I have," Dro drawled. "It's occupied quite a bit of my time over the last few days. I've come up with multiple scenarios to get the answers I want, Mayhew. Being sixty-five and overweight doesn't work in your favor. You won't be able to withstand prolonged interrogation. Now, tell me where she is."

"Reyes, I had nothing to do with it," he blubbered.

He hit him again.

Alistair spit out blood. "Why would I harm her? Lola works for me and is a great employee. I'd be a fool to mess that up. Look, I'll admit, I've had it out for your family from day one, and I've gone out of my way to undermine your father's standing in the business community, and purposefully stuck it to Santiago, but—"

"I already know all this." Dro grabbed him by the shirt. "Stop wasting my time and tell me what I want to know," he roared.

"I swear to you. I didn't kidnap her."

"Then, you know who did." He slid up a chair across from Alistair before he retrieved a bag by the desk. He took out a pair of industrial gloves and slid them on. Next, he pulled a vial from his pocket and sat down.

"What's that?" Mayhew asked, fear causing his voice to shake and be higher in tone than normal. "Truth serum? Good, I'll be happy to take it because I didn't kidnap my employee. Think about it. What's my motivation?"

"To get to me," Dro interjected. He popped the cork on the vial in his hand. "Remember? Any chance you get to stick it to a Reyes. And this isn't truth serum. That stuff doesn't work, anyway. Admit it, we were closing in on your operation, and you needed something that would get my attention. Well, you got it, Mayhew—and I've got yours," Dro smiled, but it held no warmth.

"What is that?" he repeated.

"Acid."

"What?" Alistair roared, trying his best to shrink back into his chair. "Bloody hell, are you crazy? What are you planning to do with that?"

"Isn't it obvious?"

Struggling against his restraints, Alistair pleaded. "Alejandro, stop this. I swear to you, I don't know who took Lola, but it wasn't me."

He held the bottle over Alistair's leg. "We'll see."

"Okay, okay. I'll tell you whatever you want to know."

"Why did you bug Lola?"

I was asked to," he said truthfully. "Lewis Wingate is a business partner of mine. He's gotten in over his head. *We* have gotten in, he corrected. We're businessmen, Alejandro. We saw a few opportunities to expand our interests Internationally. We jumped on it, but things started going south. Our new associates started making demands, using our warehouses to move other shipments that we weren't allowed to see or verify. I tried to distance myself from them, but Lewis won't part ways with them. He's in too deep."

"What about you?"

"Yes, I want nothing more than to get out of these entrapments while

I still have my reputation and my life. I'm many things, Reyes, but I'm not a kidnapper. I bugged her because I was hoping that I could get some leverage to negotiate a cease-fire. They threatened my son too, Alejandro, to try and keep me in line. As long as I toe the line, he stays out of harm's way. If I don't, they'll find ways to turn up the heat."

"This is all well and good, but I need names. I need possible locations of where they could be hiding Lola. I also need to know the hierarchy, Mayhew. Who took a hit out on Khalil, who is pulling everyone's strings, and what's his endgame?

"Dro, stand down," Daron warned, adjusting his fedora hat as he rushed in with his team.

"Not happening," Dro through over his shoulder.

"Help me," Mayhew cried. "He's lost it. I told you I didn't touch her. If you're so concerned about Lola, why not ask your brother and uncle where she is?"

Dro became deathly still. "You'd better start talking, or you'll have a disability for the rest of your life."

"You want to find Lola? Ask them," Alistair demanded, keeping a laser focus on the vial dangling from Dro's hand. "I'm done taking the heat for stupid men's ambitions. First Wingate runs amuck, now those two."

"You're lying."

"Am I?"Alistair snapped. "Why would I lie about something you can prove? If you don't believe me, check my cell phone. I've got plenty of text messages from the lot of them. They've partnered with Lewis, but I knew nothing about their plans. Maybe they had something to do with Lola's disappearance. I'm not going to jail or getting maimed for a crime I didn't commit."

"Dro, this has to stop," his brother calmly replied. "If he knew something, don't you think the threat of acid would've made him turn on anyone to save himself? Think, buddy. Don't do this. We'll sort this out, but not by torture."

In a split second, one of the men wrapped an arm around Dro's neck to try to pull him away. Breaking the hold, Dro threw the man over his head and onto the floor. Two men rushed him from both sides.

He slipped their hold and knocked them to the ground. Three other men took their place. "Get them out of my way, or they get hurt."

Daron held up a stun gun and pointed it at Dro's chest. "Don't make me do this."

"Dro." Shaz ran in from the doorway. "Daron, wait—"

Pain exploded from Dro's chest and blasted to every nerve in his body before it was lights out.

# CHAPTER 24

Dro opened his eyes to find himself in the Castle and stretched out on one of the guest beds in the Hyde Park wing of the Castle. But more importantly, Khalil was sitting right next to him; a worried expression covered his face.

"Welcome back, my son."

"Khalil," he croaked before trying to sit up. He immediately regretted the action and sank back against the pillows. An overwhelming heat engulfed him and breathing became difficult.

"Stay still," Khalil commanded and Dro complied. "You have been out for a while."

"From a taser? Unlikely."

"Indeed it is. Jai gave you something to help you sleep."

"I don't need to sleep," he snapped, gripping into the mattress. "I need to find my woman."

Khalil reached over and took his hands. "You have to be patient and trust the process. I know you want to be out there leading the search, but you are a wreck and not good for anyone under the circumstances."

"That wasn't their choice to make."

"No, it was mine," Khalil countered in a calm voice. "Dro, you have always been one of the Kings who had an edge. You have a single-minded determination when it comes to making things happen. It is a trait you have had since I first met you at school. I knew you would succeed at any task I put before you—but not at your peril, Victor Alejandro Reyes."

Khalil leaned closer. "I heard about what happened at Mayhew's house earlier. My son, you cannot let the need for revenge overtake you. We do what it takes to defeat evil and keep people safe because that is what we do. You were always capable, Dro, but you were *never* cruel."

Dro bristled. It wasn't what he wanted to hear, but he couldn't disagree with Khalil. He'd felt himself slipping into a dark space but was powerless to find solid footing to return. Lola touched that part of him that brought light, love and so much more. His family was a sort of anchor, but they were nothing like her.

"There are eight other Kings of the Castle for a reason. We have built-in safety protocols in place so that you all keep each other safe." He squeezed Dro's hand. "Each of you is irreplaceable and worth more to me than any mission. Even more than finding the men who tried to kill me and my son."

"I know," Dro whispered and saw Jai enter the room from his peripheral vision.

"Good. Now, like you have been there for them, I ask that you trust your brothers to bring her back in a way that doesn't put you in a dark place. That is no longer who you are, my son." He slowly exhaled, locking a steely gaze with Dro. "Missions in the past have required … how shall I say it … *necessary* measures and they were for a good cause. But now we—you—must embrace a different path, my son."

Dro bowed his head in agreement.

"Each of the Kings will have a woman who can rule in their own right," Khalil said, taking Dro's hand in his as Jai moved closer. "I plan to schedule a series of meetings with each of your women, sharing the foundation and premise of the Castle and seeing how they feel they might take part."

"You mean, work with us?" Dro said, shaking his head. "That's too dangerous."

Khalil gave a low, throaty chuckle. "They have their own path. Sometimes theirs will align with yours, and sometimes they will walk alone. Either way, they, especially your stubborn mate, need to understand the depths of what you do. Coming from you, they can downplay the meaning. Coming from me, they will assuredly understand. Then they will choose what path they wish to take for themselves."

Dro inhaled and let it out slowly, trying to keep his focus and remain alert until news of Lola came to light. He felt the prick of the needle only after it was too late to protest. "Jai, why…" The sting of betrayal was so strong it almost brought him to tears.

"Your biorhythms are all over the place," Jai protested, placing his hand across Dro's forehead. "Daron gave me access to the app that tracks our health. You developed a fever. With your immune system lowered, it is possible you contracted a virus from somewhere. It has not broken yet and it was so high you were staggering and slurring your words. You were in no condition to go after Lola's abductors. We are. We've got your back, my brother."

"But I thought you said you didn't want us in a dark place." Dro protested, putting a gaze of Khalil. "These aren't simple men. It's going to take getting a little dirty."

"I did not want you in a dark place," Khalil countered. "I have not had that conversation with Daron … yet."

Dro was filled with some semblance of relief behind those words as he tried to force his breathing to remain even. The struggle to do something so simple was so profound he felt…weightless.

"Try to get some more rest," Khalil said, placing a hand on Dro's head as Jai moved in closer. "When you awake, the woman you love will be back." Then he smiled. "I must say, Lola Samuels, is a remarkable woman. She is a great fit for you. The tether for your kite."

Dro looked surprised. "How do you know of her?"

"I know all," Khalil replied with a warm smile. "I also know that sometimes, the fixer needs fixing."

"You may be right," Dro murmured before drifting off into an exhausted sleep.

# CHAPTER 25

A few hours later, Vikkas walked down the corridor to the guest suites. When he made it to Dro's room, he silently turned the doorknob, opened the door, and poked his head inside. When he saw the made-up bed without an occupant, he shook his head and quietly pulled the door closed again.

When Dro walked through the back door and into his kitchen, he closed his eyes and soaked in the silence. The fact that he felt like he'd been gone a considerable amount of time only reiterated how he'd been sleepwalking through the last few days of his life since Lola disappeared. The true meaning behind it was clear to him.

When he glided down the hallway and past the living room, he skidded to a halt at the commotion he observed. The place looked as though he'd stepped straight into the campaign office of a political candidate, and now his home was loud, cell phones were ringing, people talking, and amid the crowd were his parents.

"Mamá. Papá," he said, his expression filled with incredulity. "What are you doing here?"

Valentina rushed over and gathered him in a fierce hug. "Where do you think we'd be, *Hijo*? With Lola getting kidnapped, our place was here by your side, of course. Though we haven't met her, we love her already. Maggie and Hugh have told us so much about her. Plus, if she's important to you, she's important to us."

His voice shook with emotion when he thanked them again for coming. When he glanced up and saw Esteban and Santiago walking into the room, Dro sprung into action.

Launching himself at his brother, he wrapped his hands around his neck. "How dare you two be here in my home after what you've done."

"Alejandro, what is the meaning of this?" His father asked in Spanish. "Release your brother."

"He betrayed me," he shot back. "So did Uncle Santiago. Where is she, Esteban? If you don't answer, so help me, I'll choke it out of you."

"Dro, stop," he heard from behind him. "You're making a mistake."

The second he heard Lola's voice, the anger dissipated from him like winds leaving a sail. He rolled off his brother and jumped to his feet. They both rushed across the room at the same time and didn't stop until they were in each other's arms.

"You're here," he breathed against the top of her head.

"Yes, I am. Dro, I've missed you. I—" Lola was unable to finish her sentence because Dro was kissing her as though he hadn't seen her in years.

She hung on for dear life and reveled in being in his arms after such a traumatic separation. When they broke apart, each had tears of joy in their eyes. It was then that he spotted Daron, Shaz, and Jai behind her, along with Alexa, Gray, and several members of his security team. They had brought her home. Khalil said to trust them, and that trust was well placed. Dro was overwhelmed by emotion. Glancing at Lola, his gaze traveled across her body as though taking inventory to ensure himself that she was there and unharmed.

She wore a gray and white striped jersey dress and white canvas shoes. He assumed they must have stopped at her house before arriving. She was thinner, had dark circles under her eyes, and looked about as worn out as he felt. To him, she was as beautiful as she'd ever been.

He wanted to hold on to her forever and hide her away until he'd drank his fill, but he saw his parents anxiously waiting for an introduction. With his arm firmly planted at her waist, he ushered her over to meet his parents.

While they were exchanging greetings, he went back over to his fellow Kings.

He hugged each one. "Thank you," he said to all of them. "You saved her life—and mine." Khalil's words had taken root. Dro was well aware that he would have ended quite a few lives behind this.

"It was our pleasure," Daron said, speaking up for everyone. "We had to get her home safe, Dro. You were starting to look like the walking dead."

"That was preferable to his first look that meant he was going to *make* someone dead," Gray observed.

He clapped each of them on the back again before seeking out Esteban.

"Explain."

"See, what had happened was…"

Dro inhaled, balling his fists by his side.

"Uncle Santiago and I were trying to help," he said in a rush of words. "By pretending to break ranks with you under the guise of wanting a larger piece of the pie, we were able to meet with a few of the key players, Alejandro. They believed we were in business for ourselves and would do our part to bring down the Kings of the Castle so we could step in and assume a dual-ownership role."

"They believed you'd sold me out?"

"Yes. Khalil recruited us," Santiago added, joining the conversation. "He provided us with enough names, bogus intel, and credentials to be believable."

Dro digested that information. "You two were double agents?"

"Yes. After Lola was taken, Mayhew contacted Khalil, and the two of them enacted a cease-fire and worked together to bring Lola home."

"I almost killed him," Dro confessed, his expression grim. "If it weren't for my brothers over there, I would have."

"So I heard," Esteban replied. "I'm glad you didn't. Considering how much help he's been in providing details on the hierarchy of power, his demise would've been bad."

"I still don't understand why Alistair decided to help us," Dro crossed his arms over his chest. "What was in it for him?"

"They threatened Shawn." Esteban placed a hand on Dro and motioned for him to go into the kitchen. "They decided he was too soft for them to trust Alistair with more responsibilities, contacts and shipments. They thought that his son could potentially be a weak link that needed to be removed. That's when Alistair broke ranks and contacted Khalil."

"So what Mayhew was saying when I interrogated him was true. All this was happening right under my nose?"

Esteban patted his brother on the shoulder. "In all fairness, you have been a bit out of your mind since Lola was taken."

Dro's gaze zeroed in on her across the room. She looked up and their eyes connected. They smiled at each other, and his heart constricted in his chest. "I'll be out of my mind about her for the rest of my life."

"Trust me, we know," his brother teased. "I'm just glad we got her home safe. She's a wonderful fit for you, baby brother."

"So, I've been told."

He reached for Esteban and held him close. "Thank you. I owe you my life."

"I'm glad I could help. I mean that, Alejandro. Everyone wants to see you happy. You deserve it."

Santiago stepped forward. "You've worked all these years tirelessly to fix other people's problems, and lives for the better. Especially mine. It's your turn, nephew."

He hugged them fiercely before shaking his brother and uncle's hand. He nodded at them, not trusting his voice, Dro sauntered over to Lola's side. He whispered in her ear, "I need to be alone with you."

She returned his openly heated look. "Lead the way."

"Everyone," he said loudly. "Lola and I would like to thank each one of you for playing a part in bringing her home safely. I can't tell you enough how much each of you means to me and how I'm eternally grateful for the role you all played in returning the woman I love to my side."

Lola squeezed his hand. "You love me?" she whispered, eyes wide with wonder.

"A hole was ripped out of my heart the moment you disappeared," Dro replied, stroking a finger down her face. "It wasn't complete again until you walked through that door. So yes, Lola Samuels. I love you. Desperately, completely and irrevocably. *Mi, Reina.*"

She kissed him deeply. "And I love you, Alejandro Reyes, King of Hyde Park."

On their way past, he stopped over to the Kings and said, "I'm going to be off the grid for a few days, so bad guys and crime will have to do without me."

"Do not worry, brother. We have got you. You two have fun," Jai promised.

# CHAPTER 26

An hour later, everyone in the house had settled down, and Lola and Dro were stretched out on a chaise lounge on his private balcony. The soft sounds of night wafted around them.

Lola inhaled deeply. "After the last few days, I don't care if I'm never alone again."

"Good to know, because my family is rather large," he teased. "You should have no problem fitting in."

She laughed and snuggled closer into his side. They laid there in companionable silence for a while before she said, "Dro?"

"Yes, *Reina?*"

"This isn't over yet, is it?"

"No," he answered truthfully. "But we have enough ammunition now to finish cleaning house and doing some serious damage on several fronts. We're nearly done with taking on the direct enemies that Khalil and the Castle has. Then the real work begins."

"Do you know who kidnapped me?"

He tensed. "I've narrowed down the suspects. And when I find them, their house of cards will be the first one I topple over."

"I'm glad," she said vehemently. "Every one of them needs to pay for what they're doing to innocent people for the sake of money and power."

"They will, Lola. That I promise you." Suddenly, he stood. "I'll be right back."

"Wait, I was comfortable," she complained, with a flirty pout.

"And you will be again," he called from the bedroom.

When he returned, he reclaimed his spot next to her but straddled the chaise lounge instead.

"I wanted to find the perfect time for this. I thought it was the night I asked you over for dinner, but it didn't go as planned."

"No, it didn't," she said sadly.

He reached out and caressed her cheek. "But one thing I've learned recently is that life's not promised to anyone. We have to make the most of the time we have because frankly, Lola, any day could be our last." He kissed her with slow, patient reverence. "I thought I'd lived through and experienced every trial I could in my life. I take chances every day. Some work in my favor, some don't. I court danger and I pat myself on the back for my ingenuity when I solve problems and save the day. My life was predictable, orderly chaos—until the day I lost you," his voice shook with emotion.

"Lola, my whole, organized little piece of the universe turned upside down. For the first time in life, my heart unraveled my mind, the day turned into night, and up was down. Nothing made sense, except that I did not rest until you were back at my side, and if I had to leave a path of destruction in my wake to find you, then so be it. That's how dark a place I was in without you. It was Khalil that showed me that I had to restore the order in my life and ease my storm."

She cried in earnest. "Dro."

"For the first time ever, I had to step aside and trust others to get the job done because I couldn't. I knew one thousand percent that I loved you, and would for eternity. Lola, you are the one person in this world that I can't live without because *You* ease my storm.

When he pulled back, he held a ring between his thumb and index finger.

"Dro," she cried, wiping the tears from her eyes with the top of her shirt so she could see it. "Yes."

He laughed. "Sweetheart, I haven't asked you yet."

"Well, hurry up, because my answer is yes. It will always be yes."

"Lola Elizabeth Samuels, will you spend the rest of your life by my side? Will you marry me?"

"Yes, Victor Alejandro Reyes, King of Hyde Park, I will marry you." She was crying in earnest now. "I love you."

He slid the three-carat oval sapphire and diamond engagement ring onto her finger. Lola was not surprised that it fit perfectly.

"I love you, mi Reina, y mi amora."

She threw her arms around him and held on for dear life. "I'm so blessed to have you in my life, Dro. You are it for me because *you* are the one person that I can't live without." Lola placed her hands on either side of his face. "I want to show you in every way possible that as of tonight, we are one."

He stood and helped her to her feet before sweeping her up into his arms. He carried her back to the bedroom and sat her down in the middle of his bed. Dro knelt in front of her. For timeless moments, they stared into each other's eyes.

"I want this to be perfect," she whispered.

He took her hand, kissed her palm, and placed it over his heart. "It already is."

In one swift movement, Lola melted into his arms. Dro held her tight before leaning her back on the bed. He reached up and removed the scrunchy holding her hair in a ponytail. It cascaded around her face.

"I look a fright," she said subconsciously.

"So do I."

She leaned in and blew her warm breath across his neck, then kissed it. "Your pulse has quickened."

He smiled at the reference. "That's because you're cutting off my air supply."

This time, her fingers traced a path down his jawline and rested on his chest above his heart. "Your skin is flushed and warm to my touch."

"I could be about to pass out from lack of oxygen."

She leaned in and stared into her eyes as best as she could in the dimly lit room. "Your pupils are dilated."

"That's because you're two inches in front of me. Anybody's eyes would be at this close range."

They shared a laugh at their running joke before Lola pulled his long-sleeved shirt up and over his head. She touched his skin and traced a path along his chest.

"Tonight, I want to commit every square inch of your body to memory."

His eyes smoldered with desire. He lobbed his discarded shirt over the side of the bed, followed a few seconds later by Lola's dress. "Me first."

* * *

A few hours later, Dro's cell phone pulsed a steady beat on the nightstand. His free arm snaked out and retrieved it. He blinked several times before attempting to read the text message. He read it twice to be sure.

"Great," he muttered.

It took him a moment to extricate himself from the bed because he didn't want to disturb Lola. He retrieved the pile of discarded clothes, padded to the bathroom, then to his closet to get dressed. When he returned, he grabbed his cell phone and went around to Lola's side of the bed.

Dro smiled. He loved the sound of that. Dro knelt next to the bed. He kissed the bridge of her nose. "Sweetheart, I'm sorry, but there's an emergency meeting at the Castle."

She stirred before saying, "Okay."

"I'll be back as soon as I can."

"Okay. I love you. Need shoes."

Dro's chest shook with mirth. He doubted she'd even know he was gone. He gave her a quick peck on the lips and walked soundlessly out of the room.

* * *

Dro entered the Castle's boardroom. The meeting was convened to drill down the list of suspects in Khalil's shooting. Sitting in one of the leather executive chairs, he opened his laptop to take notes. He stifled a yawn.

"I know you're supposed to be out of pocket for the next few days," Vikkas began. "We won't hold you any longer than necessary, brother."

"I appreciate that," Dro murmured before taking a sip of his coffee.

"Rough night?" Shaz winked.

Grant chuckled. "Don't you mean rough sex?"

"No, and no," Dro replied. "I got engaged last night."

There was a hearty round of congratulations from his brothers and hugs that made him smile.

"Oh man, sorry to have gotten you out of bed with your new bride-to-be."

He yawned and took a sip of the coffee he'd brought with him. "The sooner I get back, the better, so let's get this moving along."

Daron did a doubletake. "Whoa, Dro. You've broken a streak. Hasn't it been at least a—"

"No."

Shaz leaned forward in his chair. "Was it—"

"Not telling."

Grant dropped the pen he was holding. When Dro glanced up, the entire group was staring at him with shocked expressions.

Dro shook his head. "Really?"

"That's what we're saying," Reno chuckled. "Normally, you're the first one to brag about his exploits." He made a show of looking at the papers in front of him. "Interesting."

Shaz clapped him on the back. "Way to go, man. I'm proud of you. Show's real will-power, commitment and dedication to your fiancée."

Dro rolled his eyes upward. "Thanks, I think."

"Well, we know what won't be blue at that wedding," Kaleb joked.

After a raucous round of laughter and the evil eye from Dro, Vikkas cleared his throat and called them to order.

"Alderman Knight from Lincoln Park has been crossed off," Grant said, lifting a glass to his lips, taking a sip of wine.

Shaz shifted his locs over his shoulder. "Bennett is off, but he may have information that could lead us to the person." Bennet was an alderman of Evanston who had been involved in shady adoptions.

"Who else do we have on left on the list?" Daron asked, pulling out a tablet.

"Suarez," Dwayne answered, referring to the crooked alderman from Lawndale.

"Najan is still on my list," Vikkas added, his fingers angrily tapping the glossy conference table. Probably because he still wanted to wring his uncle's neck after what he'd pulled at his wedding that created a firestorm of drama that rocked the entire family.

Jai, who was also directly impacted by Najan's actions, nodded in agreement as he moved toward the circular table, dropping into the navy chair next to Vikkas.

"What about Jeremiah aka J-Killa and Frank Maddox?" Dro asked, turning to Kaleb and Reno. "Both were Sovereign Kings. Frank Maddox was responsible for pushing drugs and gangs in the Chatham area. Jeremiah ran a criminal enterprise and security for several aldermen who paid him to protect their families. The man was looking to expand his enterprise in the South Shore area."

"We can rule them out," Reno replied, scrolling through his cell phone. "Nothing new turned up when they were arrested."

"But we should look into a connection between J-Killa and the shooter. Maybe he referred him to the mastermind," Kaleb added.

Shaz stood, heading to the wooden credenza that held an array of drinks and sandwiches.

"Grant, what about the former medical director?" Dro asked, shaking his head as Shaz loaded several sandwiches from the platter onto a plate. "Shaz, you're going to leave some of those for us, my brother?"

Shaz did something so uncharacteristic that everyone bowled over with laughter. He stuck out his tongue out like a toddler. Then he joined in their laughter as well.

"Dr. Fowler definitely needs a closer look," Grant answered when the humor died down, causing Jai to nod. "He had verbally threatened Khalil when Daron's security team escorted him off the premises. There's something in those medical vaults that he's willing to kill for.

"The Knights are helping me to inventory everything," Jai said over the rim of his wineglass. "We're uncovering what I can only call miracles in that place. I'm telling you, we are sitting on billions. All because Khalil wanted to honestly find cures to diseases that the industry is not being truthful about."

"Billons?" Shaz said, frowning.

"Maybe more," Grant said, then asked Jai permission to share what had happened with his uncle a few weeks ago.

"Maybe we've been looking at this all wrong," Dro said. "It's always been said that we need to follow the money. Dr. Fowler could have simply stolen what was there or tapped into his databases remotely before we figured things out. Those gunshots that Khalil sustained, that seemed personal. Very personal."

Dro typed in a note to continue looking into Najan, Dr. Fowler, the politicians, and Gaurav. He didn't want to bring up the subject with Jai. It was too soon rule him out because of his newly-found blood relationship with Khalil, Jai, and Aashna, Jai's mother.

"Give a quick update on any new information." Dro glanced down to check his phone for the confirmation he and Daron were waiting for. "Let's see if we make any other connections."

The conversation focused on the Castle's recent discoveries. While Dro didn't have clear intel on who was the mastermind behind the attack, there was a major lead on the shooter.

Daron stood and looked at Dro. "It's time."

They packed up their computers and swiftly left the meeting. Dro was anxious to get back to Lola but he was excited that everyone's hard work paid off. They'd finally be able to take down the shooters.

# CHAPTER 27

Dro entered the space quietly walking behind a man with a salt-n-pepper comb-over as they passed a guard armed with an assault rifle. Neither man could see him because both he and Daron were wearing the Emperor's Suit device that made them "appear" invisible to the naked eye.

"About time," the guard greeted the man who arrived to take his place.

"Sorry I'm late," he replied before settling in behind a black podium against an exposed brick wall.

They put distance between them and the guards as they moved toward the opening at the end of the hallway. They had followed the money trail, along with the ballistics report from the second shooter's gun. Both led them to Gino Greer, a gun for hire.

Dro had unsuccessfully searched Greer's home for the weapon used to shoot Khalil, but it wasn't there. He reasoned that he could still be using it.

He followed Daron into the office. The area was cluttered with paperwork, piled on top of the desk and the cabinet lining the sides of the wall.

Dro noted that people would think the man was a legitimate furniture store salesman instead of selling illegal services.

Gino had settled into a brown leather chair with his back to the entrance. He faced the wall lined with security monitors. Puffs of smoke filled the air from the pale man's cigar. Dro positioned himself close to the wooden desk.

Dro turned off the device and slowly materialized into view. "Tell me, Gino. Is it a good day to die?"

The man whipped around in his chair and found himself staring down into the muzzle of Dro's Sig Sauer, nine-millimeter pistol.

"How quickly we get the answer to that question will depend on whether or not you lie to us," Daron retorted, leaning on the file cabinet near the desk.

Gino's cigar fell out of his mouth, and miraculously onto the black astray on the desk. "How the hell did you get in?" His brown eyes resembled saucers as he stared past beyond Dro's shoulder. Suddenly, his fearful expression morphed into a smug glare.

"That's a question, not an answer, but how is irrelevant," Dro snapped. The urge to yank Gino out of the chair, sprawl him across the desk and beat him down was overwhelming. Only Khalil's voice in his head held him at bay. *You were never cruel, Dro.*

"Today's your lucky day. We're here and ready to make you a deal. Your freedom for information on who hired you to kill Khalil Germaine."

"You have no power here." Gino stood giving Dro and Daron defiant stare.

Dro's eyes dropped to the weapons on Gino's hip. He recognized them immediately as the same type of guns used at the Castle shooting.

He raised his pistol. "Time for you to know what it feels like to have your personal domain invaded and then get shot down."

"Killing someone in cold blood." Gino snickered. "That's not the kind of man you are." He lowered himself back into the chair, shuffle papers on the desk. "Get out of here."

"You're sure that's your final answer?" Daron asked, aiming his Beretta at Gino's head.

"If these are your best intimidation tactics, you've hardly left me shaking in my boots." Gino retrieved the cigar from out of the ashtray and took a long drag before blowing smoke in Dro's face. He smiled as he returned it to the receptacle.

"You have less than five minutes to leave before my men arrive for a meeting. Three minutes after that, I'll be dragging your dead bodies out the door."

"Not in this lifetime." Dro squeezed the trigger. Twice.

The man's bushy brow raised in surprise. He grunted before his hands went to his knees. Blood seeped through his fingers from both places where he'd been shot. His surprised expression etched on his face before his reared back in the leather desk chair — his anguished screams echoing around the room. "You shot me," he yelled. "I can't believe you shot me."

"Next time, I'll aim a little higher. You'll be able to walk again when those first gunshots heal, but one more shot, and you'll be singing soprano instead of bass."

Gino's eyes widened and his bloody hands gestured to the laptop on the desk.

With limited time to work, Dro rushed over to the screen, whipping the laptop around as Gino gave him the codes needed to retrieve the information they were looking for. Daron rushed to the security system on the back wall. Something else in the office would lead them to the mastermind behind the assassination attempt. Dro was confident of that.

He glanced at the man slumped in the brown chair, passed out from the pain of two busted kneecaps. Jason Stone was on the way with a few agents to sweep the place and round up Greer's team.

Gino Greer was going to be shocked when he woke up in police custody and was charged with the attempted murder of Khalil and Vikkas.

# CHAPTER 28

The next morning when Lola and Dro came downstairs, they were greeted by his family at the breakfast table. When his mother spotted Lola's engagement ring, she threw up her arms in excitement, kissed them both and said to Lola, "I have to call your mother right. We already have some grand ideas."

When Victor and Esteban saw Dro, they offered their congratulations, as well.

Esteban hugged his brother. "I see the streak has ended."

"*Silencio*," Dro replied.

Victor engulfed Lola in his arms. "Welcome to our family, Lola. May the Lord bless you both richly and abundantly."

He released her and went to kiss his wife on the cheek. Something about his words caused her to lean in closer to Dro.

"When he says abundantly, how abundant does he mean?"

Esteban leaned in, too. "Abundantly abundant." He winked. "I should warn you that we Reyes men are *extremely* virile."

She turned to Dro, who was trying his best not to laugh. He made a muscle and blew her a kiss. Heat suffused Lola's face as she tried not to laugh.

"We must have a special dinner to celebrate," Valentina announced.

"Mom, I plan to throw a huge engagement party for Lola with friends and family as soon as we can pull it together."

"That's wonderful, *Hijo*," she told him. "But tonight, we will have our traditional family dinner."

Lola glanced over at her new fiancé. "How often do members of your family get married?"

"Not often," he chuckled. "But when we do, the first night as an engaged couple is spent with a huge dinner with the bride and groom-to-be's family."

"Seriously?"

They both looked over to find his mother writing furiously on a notepad she'd found in a kitchen drawer.

"Seriously," he confirmed.

"But my parents aren't due to come for a visit for another few weeks."

He wrapped an arm around her shoulders. "Sweetheart, it's no problem. We'll fly them in."

"Tonight?"

"Sure. You have anything else planned?"

She shoved him playfully. "Okay, I'll call them and invite them to fly in for the engagement dinner."

"And Travers and El?"

"Oh, yes," Dro said, smacking a hand to his forehead. "El will kill me if she misses out. That woman has been my right hand since I could remember. Travers is a little different when it comes to decorum and boundaries, but I think he'd love to come. He's family, just like El."

Though it was last minute, he agreed with his mother that it should be in grand style. To that end, he called one of his favorite caterers, *Magnolia Maven*. When the owner answered, he said hello, and handed his mother the telephone.

After breakfast, Dro announced that he and Lola were going to get lost for a few hours. He drove Lola to a Hyde Park neighborhood favorite, the Museum of Science and Industry in Jackson Park. It was between Lake Michigan and The University of Chicago.

They held hands as they strolled through the exhibits. Dro was about to walk past the Giant Dome Theater, but Lola stopped him.

"Oh no you don't. I want to see the Secrets of the Universe."

The screen was massive and luckily, they found two seats available toward the back of the theater.

Next on Dro's list was the 57th Street Books. While he was perusing the cookbooks, Lola headed for the general interest titles. When they met up again, Dro had one book, Lola had four. He took the books from her and carried them to checkout.

"Uh, what do all of these books have Bride in the title?

"I couldn't resist," she said excitedly.

"Next, they took a stroll at Oakwood Beach, also known as 41st Street Beach.

"I love this city," Lola raved.

"Speaking of love, I guess we should decide when we're getting married."

"True. How about an Autumn wedding?"

Dro pondered it for a moment. "I'm good with that. I think you'd make a beautiful fall bride—actually, a bride at any season. Just so long as you're *my* bride."

She kissed him. "That was sweet. Thank you."

"You're welcome, soon-to-be *Señora* Reyes."

Lola leaned into his side. "I love the sound of that, *Señor* Reyes."

He wrapped an arm around her shoulder. "I love you."

His cell phone pulsed. Checking the number, he frowned. "Hang on a sec, sweetheart. Hey, Daron, what's up?"

"You aren't going to believe this."

Dro shook his head. "What now? Whatever it is, the answer is no," he said, firmly. "You know I'm trying to relax and enjoy Lola being back, and my family's visit. I'm not hopping on a plane, threatening to kill anybody, or fixing anything, Daron. It's my day off."

"That's going to have to wait. Just hang on a minute, and you'll understand why."

Frowning, he clenched his jaw while he waited for Daron to bring him up to speed. He hung up and turned to Lola. "We're closing in on the man who tried to kill Khalil and Vikkas."

His phone rang again. This time it was Jai and Daron.

"Dude, I just got off the phone with you."

"Just hear me out. You'll be glad you did."

Dro's expression grew more surprised by the minute. Finally, he said, "You know that's a tall order, right?" After hearing what Jai had in mind.

After hanging up, he brought Lola up to speed on the rest of the details.

"That's great news, Dro," she said excitedly.

"Baby, do you mind if we post-pone our dinner until tomorrow?"

"No, of course not," she said quickly. "We'll just have to convince your mom."

Dro kissed her lips and then shimmied his shoulders and sang, "We are family. I've got all my brothers with me."

She covered her ears in mock horror. "Please don't quit your day job."

"I can't believe we're doing this. I need a new occupation."

"Oh please," Lola giggled. "You're just fishing for compliments. You're amazing at what you do, and everyone knows it. Let me know if I can help in any way."

He flashed her one of his high-wattage smiles. "Great. You can break the news to my mother," he said before sprinting down the beach.

"Oh no, you don't," she called out, racing after him.

* * *

"You know, I was thinking."

"Ouch, here comes trouble," Dro teased and she punched him hard enough for a true "Ouch."

"Jai and Temple had one of the most beautiful weddings I've ever attended," Lola said before yawning. It was almost dawn when they returned to the house. They tiptoed upstairs, careful not to wake the household.

Exhausted, they got out of their clothes and into pajamas in record time. Lola was the first to get into the bed. She snuggled down into the plush covers and sighed aloud.

"Yes, it was wonderful," he agreed.

"And Shaz *was* crying."

"Twice," Dro confirmed with a quiet laugh. "I'm never going to let him live it down. Allergies my ass."

"I'd like to have a simple wedding like theirs."

Dro hauled her up against him and buried his face in her neck. "Whatever you want. Girl, you know I can provide," he crooned and then finished the rest of the R&B song, relishing Lola's smile.

"You have an amazing voice," Lola whispered, giving him a kiss.

"I can't wait until I've officially made you my wife. It'll be the best day of my life."

"I don't know, you've had quite a life," Lola said quickly.

Dro used his finger to tilt her face up to his. "I have lived an extraordinary life, Lola. Full of danger, intrigue, luxuries, and plenty of toys. But the one thing that I didn't have was someone to love me for me." He buried his face in her neck for a kiss. "Sure, my family is close-knit, and they'll always love me, but having someone in my corner through good times and bad, that's my partner in life is what matters most. That's what I never thought I'd be blessed enough to find. My whole life has been working to make other people's lives happy and complete. I never knew how much I longed for that until I met you."

"I knew I loved you the night you showed up on my doorstep after getting shot. You picked me over a hospital. That's something a woman never forgets. Just don't make a habit of it," she teased.

"And you healed me," he said softly, taking Khalil's words to heart. "From the inside out. You've fixed the fixer, my love. My beautiful *Reina.*"

King of Hyde Park introduced you to Marena Dash and Alexa King who have their own stories releasing in 2022 and 2024

Six Days to Live

In less than a week he'll be dead…

Unless she can save him.

The poison Coulter McKendrick was injected with during a commando raid will kill him in six days. Dr. Marena Dash is Colt's only chance to live. Though Colt devastated Marena when he left her, she's determined to find the antidote to save him. And with the criminals behind the biotoxin on their trail, Colt and Marena must put their past behind them to stay alive.


From Harlequin Romantic Suspense: Danger. Passion. Drama.

**The Bodyguard's Deadly Mission**

She wants to protect women…
He needs to protect her.

Alexa King and Andrew Riker met when he trained her to be a bodyguard. Despite their simmering connection—and a few unguarded moments—she's managed to keep their relationship purely professional. But now she runs her own security business, and her latest contract puts both her and Andrew in danger. She knows she can trust Andrew with her life. Will she trust him with her heart?

From Harlequin Romantic Suspense: Danger. Passion. Drama.

# Lisa Dodson

Lisa Dodson is a National and Amazon #1 Bestselling Author and native of Washington, DC. She has written over eighteen Multicultural, Contemporary, Romantic Suspense, Sweet Romance, Clean Read, and Christian Fiction novels. A hybrid author, Lisa enjoys creating engaging storylines, strong characters with universal appeal, and a keen sense of humor. They are drawn together by love, respect, and strong family ties. In addition, Lisa loves traveling, so weaving beautiful destinations into the pages of her novels as lush backdrops or the heritage of her characters is not uncommon.

Lisa is a Business Development Manager at a technology consulting firm, a mother of two young adults, and lives in Raleigh, NC. She is avidly working on upcoming projects in multiple genres.

Her latest novel, Six Days to Live, was released in October 2022 for Harlequin Romantic Suspense. Her next novel, The Bodyguard's Deadly Mission, is now available for Pre-Order and will be released on 1/23/2024.

Lisa enjoys writing warm-your-heart stories. Her novellas, *A Summer of Stars*, her holiday-themed Sweet Romances, *A Heart for Christmas, Two Hearts for Christmas*, and *A Fiancé for Christmas,* make great reads no matter what time of the year.

Her Romantic Suspense, *Spicing Things Up*, proves that there's a time for playing it safe, but sometimes you need to spice things up!

Danger doesn't need an appointment…sometimes it just shows up! With an adoring assistant, an ambitious publicist, and jealous ex-lover vying for her attention, debut novelist, Sasha Lambert, soon finds herself at the center of a dangerous tug-of-war. *Interview with Danger* is a thrill ride that you'll want to be on!

# ABOUT THE KINGS OF THE CASTLE SERIES

Books 2-9 are standalones, no cliffhangers, and can be read in any order.

**Book 1 – Kings of the Castle**, the introduction to the series and story of King of Wilmette (Vikkas Germaine)

*USA TODAY*, *New York Times*, and National Bestselling Authors work together to provide you with a world you'll never want to leave. The Castle. Powerful men unexpectedly brought together by their pasts and current circumstances will become a force to be reckoned with. Their combined efforts to find the people responsible for the attempt on their mentor's life, is the beginning of dangerous challenges that will alter the path of their lives forever. Not to mention, they will also draw the ire and deadly intent of current Castle members who wield major influence across the globe.

Fate made them brothers, but protecting the Castle and the women they love, will make them Kings. www.thekingsofthecastle.com

*King of Chatham - Book 2 - Reno*
*King of Evanston - Book 3 - Shaz*
*King of Devon - Book 4 - Jai*
*King of Morgan Park - Book 5 - Daron*
*King of South Shore - Book 6 - Kaleb*
*King of Lincoln Park - Book 7 - Grant*
*King of Hyde Park - Book 8 - Dro*
*King of Lawndale - Book 9 - Dwayne*

*Cover design by J. L. Woodson - www.woodsonstudio.com*

# ABOUT THE KINGS OF THE CASTLE SERIES

Books 2-9 are standalones, no cliffhangers, and can be read in any order.

**Book 1 – Kings of the Castle**, the introduction to the series and story of King of Wilmette (Vikkas Germaine)

*USA TODAY*, *New York Times*, and National Bestselling Authors work together to provide you with a world you'll never want to leave. The Castle. Powerful men unexpectedly brought together by their pasts and current circumstances will become a force to be reckoned with. Their combined efforts to find the people responsible for the attempt on their mentor's life, is the beginning of dangerous challenges that will alter the path of their lives forever. Not to mention, they will also draw the ire and deadly intent of current Castle members who wield major influence across the globe.

Fate made them brothers, but protecting the Castle and the women they love, will make them Kings.

www.thekingsofthecastle.com

**King of Chatham - Book 2**

While Mariano "Reno" DeLuca uses his skills and resources to create safe havens for battered women, a surge in criminal activity within the Chatham area threatens the women's anonymity and security. When Zuri, an exotic Tanzanian Princess, arrives seeking refuge from an arranged marriage and its deadly consequences, Reno is now forced to relocate the women in the shelter, fend off unforeseen enemies of The Castle, and endeavor not to lose his heart to the mysterious woman.

### King of Evanston - Book 3

Raised as an immigrant, he knows the heartache of family separation firsthand. His personal goals and business ethics collide when a vulnerable woman stands to lose her baby in an underhanded and profitable scheme crafted by powerful, ruthless businessmen and politicians who have nefarious ties to The Castle. Shaz and the Kings of the Castle collaborate to uproot the dark forces intent on changing the balance of power within The Castle and destroying their mentor. National Bestselling Author, J.L. Campbell presents book 3 in the Kings of the Castle Series, featuring Shaz Bostwick.

### King of Devon - Book 4

When a coma patient becomes pregnant, Jaidev Maharaj's medical facility comes under a government microscope and media scrutiny. In the midst of the investigation, he receives a mysterious call from someone in his past that demands that more of him than he's ever been willing to give and is made aware of a dark family secret that will destroy the people he loves most.

### King of Morgan Park - Book 5

Two things threaten to destroy several areas of Daron Kincaid's life—the tracking device he developed to locate victims of sex trafficking and an inherited membership in a mysterious outfit called The Castle. The new developments set the stage to dismantle the relationship with a woman who's been trained to make men weak or put them on the other side of the grave. The secrets Daron keeps from Cameron and his inner circle only complicates an already tumultuous situation caused by an FBI sting that brought down his former enemies. Can Daron take on his enemies, manage his secrets and loyalty to the Castle without permanently losing the woman he loves?

**King of South Shore - Book 6**

Award-winning real estate developer, Kaleb Valentine, is known for turning failing communities into thriving havens in the Metro Detroit area. His plans to rebuild his hometown neighborhood are dereailed with one phone call that puts Kaleb deep in the middle of an intense criminal investigation led by a detective who has a personal vendetta. Now he will have to deal with the ghosts of his past before they kill him.

**King of Lincoln Park - Book 7**

Grant Khambrel is a sexy, successful architect with big plans to expand his Texas Company. Unfortunately, a dark secret from his past could destroy it all unless he's willing to betray the man responsible for that success, and the woman who becomes the key to his salvation.

**King of Hyde Park - Book 8**

Alejandro "Dro" Reyes has been a "fixer" for as long as he could remember, which makes owning a crisis management company focused on repairing professional reputations the perfect fit. The same could be said of Lola Samuels, who is only vaguely aware of his "true" talents and seems to be oblivious to the growing attraction between them. His company, Vantage Point, is in high demand and business in the Windy City is booming. Until a mysterious call following an attempt on his mentor's life forces him to drop everything and accept a fated position with The Castle. But there's a hidden agenda and unexpected enemy that Alejandro doesn't see coming who threatens his life, his woman, and his throne.

**King of Lawndale - Book 9**

Dwayne Harper's passion is giving disadvantaged boys the tools to transform themselves into successful men. Unfortunately, the minute he steps up to take his place among the men he considers brothers, two things stand in his way: a political office that does not want the competition Dwayne's new education system will bring, and a well-connected former member of The Castle who will use everything in his power—even those who Dwayne mentors—to shut him down.

## AUTHOR BIOS

**Naleighna Kai** is the *USA TODAY* Bestselling Author of Every Woman Needs a Wife, Open Door Marriage, Loving Me for Me, Slaves of Heaven and several other controversial novels. She is founder of NK Tribe Called Success, The Cavalcade of Authors, and is a publishing and marketing consultant. www.naleighnakai.com

**S. L. Jennings** is a military wife, mom of three, coffee addict, Willy Wonka enthusiast, and real-life unicorn. She's also the New York Times and USA Today Bestselling author of Taint, Fear of Falling and the Se7en Sinners Series, along with a few other titles that she's too lazy to type. She's been with her high school sweetheart for almost twenty years, and he still can't get her Subway sandwich order right. But he's cute and brings her vodka, so she keeps him around. They currently reside in Spokane, WA with their three stinky boys and their equally stinky cat. www.sljenningsauthor.com

**Martha Kennerson** is the bestselling and award-winning author who's love of reading and writing is a significant part of who she is. She uses both to create the kinds of stories that touch the heart. Martha lives with her family in League City, Texas. She believes her current blessings are only matched by the struggle it took to achieve such happiness. To find out more about Martha and her journey, visit her website at www.marthakennerson.com and you can follow her on Facebook and Twitter.

**J. L. Campbell** is an award-winning Jamaican author who has written over thirty books in several romance subgenres. Campbell, who features Jamaican culture in her stories, is a certified editor, and also writes non-fiction. Visit her on the web at www.joylcampbell.com.

National bestselling author, **Lisa Dodson** is a native of Washington D.C., and writes in the Multicultural & Interracial, Contemporary, Romantic Suspense, and Sweet Romance genres. Her memorable novels for the Harlequin's Kimani line, The Match Broker series was listed as one of 2014's Top 25 Books of the Summer, and Top 50 Best Reads. Lisa lives in Raleigh, North Carolina with her husband of twenty-two years and two teenagers, and is avidly working on book one, Alexa King: The Guardian, in her second new Romantic Suspense series, The Lady Doyen and Book 2 in the Love and Danger Series. www.lisawatson.com

**Karen D. Bradley** is a national bestselling author and screenplay writer. English and Grammar were never her strongest subjects, but as life would have it, her weakest link would become her saving grace. Writing fiction became one of her favorite forms of therapy. She has penned several contemporary fiction, suspense, and romantic suspense novels. Visit Karen on the web at www.karendbradley.com

**Janice M. Allen** is a National Bestselling Author who has always been an avid reader of fiction. She even edited the work of other authors for several years. But she gets an incomparable thrill from creating stories that entertain readers and cause them to reflect on real life issues. No Right Way To Do A Wrong Thing is her first novel, followed by her short story Cayenne. www.janicemallen.com

**London St. Charles** has always had a passion for the pen, paper, and books. She is a Chicago native who uses the Windy City as a backdrop to the romance, suspense, and contemporary fiction stories she writes. London published her debut novel, The Husband We Share in 2017 and is one of nine authors in the anthology, Sugar. She also composes an online newsletter, London Writes, that keeps readers abreast of what's going on in her world. www.londonstcharles.com

**MarZe Scott** is a lifelong resident of Ypsilanti, Michigan and Graduate of University of Michigan. A lover of all things creative, MarZé enjoys reading, free-hand illustrating, jewelry making and makeup artistry.

Known for her vivid and captivating storytelling, MarZé has been writing short stories and poems since elementary school and developed a taste in high school for writing about provocative topics like the consequences of casual sex. You can find Gemini Rising, MarZé's debut novel, and short story Next Lifetime wherever books are sold.  www.marzescott.com

## SERIES MENTORS:

**LaVerne Thompson** is a *USA Today* Bestselling, award winning, multi-published author, an avid reader and a writer of contemporary, fantasy, and sci/fi sensual romances. She loves creating worlds within and without our world. She also writes romantic suspense and new adult romance under the pen name Ursula Sinclair also a USA Today Bestselling Author. www.lavernethompson.com

**Kassanna** is a strong believer in love at first sight and happily ever afters. Writing has always been her passion but fate sometimes has other roads that must first be taken .Navigating the road less traveled was not only unexpected but in the end extremely rewarding. Her books are mainly contemporary romance but she has delved into the paranormal, fantasy, and plans on expanding into other areas as the ideas come to her. Right now she is enjoying life and seeing her works come into fruition make it that much more pleasurable especially when her books make others smile. Kassanna wouldn't have it any other way. www.flavorfullove.com